YOU ARE THE
CLASSICS

**ROBERT LOUIS STEVENSON
AND MATT LONDON**

D1397449

Penguin W

To S.L.O., an American gentleman in accordance with whose classic taste the following narrative has been designed, it is now, in return for numerous delightful hours, and with the kindest wishes, dedicated by his affectionate friend, the author.

And to R.L.S., a gentleman in his own right, it is now, in return for this invaluable lesson in adventure, and with the sincerest apologies, dedicated by his affectionate student, the other author.

PENGUIN WORKSHOP
An Imprint of Penguin Random House LLC, New York

Penguin supports copyright. Copyright fuels creativity, encourages diverse voices, promotes free speech, and creates a vibrant culture. Thank you for buying an authorized edition of this book and for complying with copyright laws by not reproducing, scanning, or distributing any part of it in any form without permission. You are supporting writers and allowing Penguin to continue to publish books for every reader.

Cover illustration by M. S. Corley

Visit us online at www.penguinrandomhouse.com.

Library of Congress Control Number: 2021005905

ISBN 9780593095911   10 9 8 7 6 5 4 3 2 1

Squire Trelawney, Dr. Livesey, and the rest of these gentlemen asked me to write down the whole particulars about Treasure Island, from the beginning to the end, keeping nothing back but the bearings of the island, and that only because there is still treasure not yet lifted. I take up my pen in the year of grace 17__ and go back to the time when my mother kept the Admiral Benbow inn and the brown old seaman with the saber cut first took up his lodging under our roof.

I remember him as if it were yesterday, as he came plodding to the inn door, his sea-chest following behind him in a hand-barrow—a tall, strong, heavy, brown man, his tarry pigtail falling over the shoulder of his soiled blue coat, his hands ragged and scarred, with black, broken nails, and the saber cut across one cheek a dirty, livid white. I remember him looking round the cover and whistling to himself as he did so, and then breaking out in that old sea-song that he sang so often afterwards:

"Fifteen men on the dead man's chest—
Yo-ho-ho, and a bottle of rum!"

He sang in a high, old tottering voice that seemed to have been tuned and broken while hoisting sails. He rapped on the door with a bit of stick like a handspike he carried, and when my mother appeared, called roughly for a glass of rum.

"This is a handy cove," the old seaman said, "and a pleasant grog-shop. Much company, lass?"

My mother told him no, very little company, the more was the pity.

"Well, then," said he, "this is the berth for me. I want bacon and eggs each morning. I'll take your best room with a window view of the sea, and you might call me captain." He threw down three or four gold pieces, looking as fierce as a commander. "You can tell me when I've worked through that."

He was a silent man by custom. All day he hung round the cove or upon the cliffs with a brass telescope; all evening he sat in a corner of the parlor next to the fire and drank rum and water very strong. Mostly he would not speak when spoken to, so I learned to let him be.

One day, he took me aside and promised me a silver fourpenny on the first of every month if I would only keep my "weather-eye open for a seafaring man with one leg" and let him know the moment he appeared.

How that one-legged man haunted my dreams, I need scarcely tell you. I saw him as a monstrous kind of creature who had never had but the one leg, and that in the middle of his body. To see him leap and run and pursue me over hedge and ditch was the worst of nightmares. In my dreams I paid dearly for that monthly silver coin.

Because my fear of the man with one leg was so profound, I was far less afraid of the captain himself than anybody else who knew him. There were nights at the inn when he would sit and sing his wicked, old, wild sea-songs, and call for glasses round and force the other trembling patrons—and Mother and me as well—to listen to his stories or be the chorus to his singing. The inn would shake with "Yo-ho-ho, and a bottle of rum," all the neighbors joining in with the fear of death upon them, and each singing louder than the other to avoid the captain's wrath.

There was only one person who dared to cross the captain; Dr. Livesey, the local physician, came late one afternoon to check up on us and take a bit of dinner. The captain was there, of course, and I remember observing the contrast of the neat, bright doctor, with his powdered wig as white as snow and his bright, black eyes and pleasant manners, with that filthy, heavy, bleared scarecrow of a pirate, sitting with his arms on the table.

Suddenly the captain began to pipe up his eternal song:

"Fifteen men on the dead man's chest—
Yo-ho-ho, and a bottle of rum!
Drink and the devil had done for the rest—
Yo-ho-ho, and a bottle of rum!"

Our regular patrons, who had grown accustomed to this nightly torture, chimed in at once. At the same moment, I observed on Dr. Livesey's face that the song did not produce an agreeable effect. He looked up for a moment quite angrily before he went on with his talk to old Taylor, the gardener.

The captain sang louder and louder, as if to indicate to the doctor that he should pay attention and join in. When Dr. Livesey showed no reaction, the captain flapped his hand upon the table before him in a way we all knew to mean *silence*. The voices stopped at once, all but Dr. Livesey's; he went on speaking as before. The captain glared at him for a while, flapped his hand again, glared still harder, and at last broke out with a villainous, low oath, "Silence, there, between decks!"

"Were you addressing me, sir?" said the doctor.

"Aye." The captain sniffed.

"Well, I have only one thing to say to you, sir," Dr. Livesey replied, "that if you keep on drinking rum, the world will soon be rid of a very dirty scoundrel!"

The old pirate's fury was awful. He sprang to his feet, drew and opened a sailor's clasp-knife, and balancing it open on the palm of his hand, threatened to pin the doctor to the wall.

As the man of the house, young though I was, it fell to me to settle rows in the establishment. On the other hand, I was but a boy, and the captain was a grown pirate mighty with drink. If I crossed him, I could end up stuck like a holiday goose. Perhaps you have begun to see where I am going with this. You have a say in the path my story takes. Yes, you, dear reader. So I ask you in this moment, what would you do if a frothing old sea-captain threatened a good man with a knife?

If you would step between them,
turn to page 39

If you would let Dr. Livesey handle it,
turn to page 86

"Don't worry, boy, Harry'll catch that rotten pirate," said Long John Silver, still holding fast to my arm. "If he were Admiral Hawke, he will pay me for the rum he owes me. He shall pay his score." He relinquished my arm. "Who did you say he was? Black what?"

"Dog, sir," said I. "Has Mr. Trelawney not told you of Black Dog? A scoundrel, he is, and he came to my home, sir. I thought he was dead."

"Truly?" cried Silver. "In my house! Ben, run and help Harry. One of those swabs, was he? Was that you drinking with him, Morgan? Step up here."

The man whom he called Morgan—an old, gray-haired, mahogany-faced sailor—came forward pretty sheepishly, chewing on his cheek.

"Now, Morgan," said Long John very sternly, "you never clapped your eyes on that Black—Black Dog before, did you, now?"

"Not I, sir," said Morgan with a salute.

"If you had been mixed up with the like of that, you would never have put another foot in my house. What was he saying to you?"

"I don't rightly know, sir," answered Morgan.

"Do you call that a head on your shoulders?" cried Long John. "Don't rightly know? Come, now, what was he talking about? Voyages? Captains? Ships? Pipe up!"

"We was a-talkin' of keel-hauling," answered Morgan.

"Keel-hauling, was you? I should keel-haul you!"

As Morgan rolled back to his seat, Silver added to me in a confidential whisper, "He's quite an honest man, Tom Morgan, only stupid. If we run down this Black Dog now, that will please Cap'n Trelawney!"

My suspicions had been thoroughly reawakened on finding Black Dog at the Spy-glass, and I watched the cook narrowly. But he was too clever for me, and by the time the two men had come back out of breath and confessed that they had lost track of Black Dog in a crowd, and been scolded like thieves, I would have testified in court to the innocence of Long John Silver.

"See here, now, Hawkins," said he. "Let me put on my old hat and we'll step along to Cap'n Trelawney, and report this here affair."

On our little walk along the quays, he made himself the most interesting companion, telling me about the different ships that we passed by, their rig, tonnage, and nationality, explaining the work that was going forward—how one was discharging, another taking in cargo, and a third making ready for sea—and every now and then telling me some little anecdote of ships or seamen or repeating a nautical phrase till I had learned it perfectly. I began to see that here was one of the best of possible shipmates.

When we got to the inn, the squire and Dr. Livesey were seated together, preparing to go aboard the schooner on a visit of inspection.

Long John told the story from first to last, with a great deal of spirit and the most perfect truth. "That was how it were, now, weren't it, Hawkins?" he would say, now and again, and I could always bear him entirely out.

The two gentlemen regretted that Black Dog had got away, but we all agreed there was nothing to be done, and after he had been complimented, Long John took up his crutch and departed.

"Well, squire," said Dr. Livesey. "I don't put much faith in your discoveries as a general thing; but that John Silver suits me very well indeed."

"The man is perfect," declared the squire.

"And now," added the doctor, "Jim may come on board with us, may he not?"

I inhaled deeply and puffed up my chest a bit when I

realized they were talking about me. Though young, I was ready for the journey.

"To be sure he may," said the squire. "Take your hat, Hawkins, and we'll see the ship."

Turn to page 94

As I waited for Squire Trelawney to send word from Bristol, I brooded over the map, committing all the details to memory and approaching the island in my fancy from every possible direction.

Weeks passed, until one fine day came a letter.

The ship is bought and fitted. She lies at anchor, ready for sea. You never imagined a sweeter schooner—a child might sail her—two hundred tons; name, Hispaniola.

I wished to hire a score of men—in case of buccaneers or the odious French—and I had great trouble finding even half a dozen who were suitable, until the most remarkable stroke of fortune brought me the very man that I required.

Long John Silver, he is called, and he has lost a leg in his country's service. He keeps a public-house and knows all the seafaring men in Bristol. I hired him to be ship's cook on the spot.

With Long John's help we got together a company of

the toughest old salts imaginable—not pretty, but tough enough
to fight a frigate. He also unearthed a very competent man for a
mate, a man named Arrow.

Do not lose an hour. Come at full speed to Bristol.

John Trelawney

You can fancy the excitement into which that letter put me. The doctor and I did not hesitate to hurry on to Bristol. The carriage that delivered the mail picked us up about dusk, and I was wedged in between Dr. Livesey and a stout old gentleman, and in spite of the swift motion and the cold night air, I must have dozed a great deal from the very first. When I opened my eyes, we were standing still before a large building in a city street in the middle of the day.

"Where are we?" I asked.

"Bristol," said the driver. "Get out."

Mr. Trelawney had taken up his residence at an inn far down the docks to oversee the work on our schooner, and as we walked along the quays we saw a great multitude of ships of all sizes and rigs and nations. In one, sailors were singing at their work; in another, there were men aloft, high over my head, hanging to threads that seemed no thicker than a spider's. I smelled the tar and salt and saw the most wonderful figureheads that had all been far over the ocean. I saw many old sailors with rings in their ears, and whiskers curled in ringlets, and tarry pigtails, and their swaggering, clumsy way of walking. If kings and archbishops had been among them,

I could not have been more delighted. And I was going to sea myself, on a schooner, with pigtailed singing seamen, bound for an unknown island, to seek for buried treasure!

While I was still in this delightful dream, we came suddenly in front of a large inn and met Squire Trelawney, all dressed out like a sea-officer, in stout blue cloth, coming through the door of the building with a smile on his face and a capital imitation of a sailor's walk.

"Here you are," he cried, "cabin-boy and ship's doctor. Bravo! Our company is complete!"

"Oh, sir," cried I, "when do we sail?"

"Sail!" said he. "We sail tomorrow!"

The squire led us in and fed us a hearty breakfast, then gave me a note addressed to John Silver, at the sign of the Spy-glass, and told me I should easily find the place by following the line of the docks and keeping a bright lookout for a little tavern with a large brass telescope for sign. I set off, overjoyed at this opportunity to see some more of the different ships and seamen, and picked my way among a great crowd of people and carts and bales, for the dock was now at its busiest, until I found the tavern in question.

It was a bright enough little place for entertainment. The sign was newly painted; the windows had neat red curtains; the floor was cleanly sanded. The doors on either side of the large, low room were open, streaming light in from outside. The customers were mostly seafaring men, and they talked so loudly that I hung at the door, afraid to enter.

As I was waiting, a man came out of a side room, and at a glance I was sure he must be Long John. His left leg was cut off close by the hip, and under the left shoulder he carried a crutch, which he managed with wonderful dexterity, hopping about upon it like a bird. He was very tall and strong, with a face as big as a ham—plain and pale, but intelligent and smiling. Indeed, he seemed in the most cheerful spirits, whistling as he moved about among the tables, with a merry word or a slap on the shoulder for his favored guests.

Now to tell you the truth, from the very first mention of Long John in Squire Trelawney's letter I had taken a fear in my mind that he might prove to be the very one-legged sailor whom I had watched for so long at the old Benbow. But one look at the man before me was enough. I had seen the captain, and Black Dog, and I thought I knew what a buccaneer was like—a very different creature, according to me, from this clean and pleasant-tempered landlord.

I walked right up to the man where he stood, propped on his crutch, talking to a customer.

"Mr. Silver, sir?" I asked, holding out the note.

"Yes, my lad," said he; "such is my name, to be sure. And who may you be?" And then as he saw the squire's letter, he seemed to give something almost like a start.

"Oh!" said he, offering his hand. "I see. You are Jim Hawkins, our new cabin-boy; pleased I am to see you."

And he took my hand in his large firm grasp.

Just then one of the customers at the far side of the room rose and made for the door. It was close by him, and he was out in the street in a moment. But his hurry had attracted my notice, and I recognized him at a glance. It was the pale, sickly man, wanting two fingers, now with a bandage on his shoulder, who had come first to the Admiral Benbow. How was this possible? I'd thought for certain he was dead, succumbed to his injuries, but he was very much alive, and at the moment, escaping.

"Oh," I cried, "stop him! It's Black Dog!"

"I don't care two coppers who he is," cried Silver. "He hasn't paid his score. Harry, run and catch him."

"I'll get him. I owe it to the captain!" I called, rushing after Long John's mate, but the innkeeper grabbed me and held me fast by the arm.

"Wait, boy! It's dangerous. Let a man go. You stay."

**If you would stay with
Long John Silver,** turn to page 6

If you would chase after Black Dog,
turn to page 147

I rode hard all the way till I drew up before Dr. Livesey's door. The house was all dark in the front. I jumped down and knocked, and the door was opened almost at once by the maid.

"Is Dr. Livesey in?" I asked.

No, she said, he had gone up to the hall to dine and pass the evening with Squire Trelawney. I hurried along, and when I arrived at the hall, a servant showed me to a great library, all lined with bookcases and busts upon the top of them, where the squire and Dr. Livesey sat, pipes in hand, on either side of a bright fire.

I had never seen the squire so near at hand. He was a tall man, over six feet high, and broad in proportion, and he had a bluff, rough-and-ready face, all coarse and reddened and lined from his long travels. His eyebrows were as black as night, and moved readily, and this gave him a look of some temper, not bad, you would say, but quick and high.

They insisted I recount my experience, and as I told my tale they forgot to smoke in their surprise and interest. When my tale was told, Squire Trelawney slapped his thigh in excitement.

"And so, Jim," said the doctor, "you have the thing that all the violence was about?"

"Here it is, sir," said I, and gave him the oilskin packet.

The doctor looked it all over, as if his fingers were itching to open it; but instead of doing that, he put it quietly in the pocket of his coat. "Squire," said he, "I mean to keep Jim Hawkins here to sleep at my house, and with your permission, I propose we should have up the cold pie and let him sup."

"As you will, Livesey," said the squire; "Hawkins has earned better than cold pie."

So a big pigeon pie was brought in and put on a side table, and I made a hearty supper, for I was hungry as a hawk.

"And now, Squire," said the doctor.

"And now, Livesey," said the squire in the same breath.

"One at a time, one at a time," said Dr. Livesey, laughing. "You have heard of this Flint, I suppose?"

"Heard of him!" cried the squire. "Heard of him, you say! He was the bloodthirstiest buccaneer that ever sailed. Blackbeard was a child compared to Flint. The Spaniards were so prodigiously afraid of him that, I tell you, sir, I was sometimes proud he was an Englishman."

"But did he have any money?" asked the doctor.

"Money!" cried the squire. "What would a rascal pirate risk his carcass for but money? Flint's whole deplorable life was about money."

"What I want to know is this: Supposing that I have here in my pocket some clue to where Flint buried his treasure, will that treasure amount to much?"

"Amount, sir!" cried the squire. "If we have the clue you talk about, I'll leave for Bristol right now, buy a ship, hire a crew, and drag you and Hawkins here across the ocean for a year to find that treasure."

"Very well," said the doctor. "Now, then, if Jim is agreeable, we'll open the packet."

The bundle was sewn together, and the doctor had to get out his instrument case and cut the stitches with his medical scissors. It contained a book and a sealed paper.

The squire and I peered over the doctor's shoulder as he opened the book. It contained events and amounts recorded over twenty years. It was the black-hearted Flint's account book, tracking all the plunder he had accumulated over his long career.

The paper had been sealed with wax in several places. The doctor opened the seals with great care, and there fell out the map of an island, with latitude and longitude, names of hills and bays and inlets, and every particular that would be needed to bring a ship to a safe anchorage upon its shores. The island was about nine miles long and five across, shaped, you might say, like a fat dragon standing up, and had two fine land-locked harbors, and a hill in the center part marked "The Spy-glass."

Most significantly, there were three crosses of red ink—two on the north part of the island, one in the southwest—and beside this last, in the same red ink, in small, neat hand, these words: "Bulk of treasure here."

"Livesey," said the squire, clapping him on the back, "congratulations, you're officially retired from the medical profession. Tomorrow I start for Bristol. In three weeks' time—three weeks!—two weeks—ten days—we'll have the best ship, sir, and the choicest crew in England. Hawkins shall come as cabin-boy. You'll make a famous cabin-boy, Hawkins. You, Livesey, are ship's doctor; I am admiral. We'll take Redruth, Joyce, and Hunter. We'll have favorable winds, a quick passage, and not the least difficulty in finding the spot, and money enough to bathe in ever after."

"Trelawney," said the doctor, "I'll go with you; so will Jim, and be a credit to the undertaking. There's only one man I'm afraid of."

"And who's that?" cried the squire. "Name the dog, sir!"

"You," replied the doctor; "for you cannot hold your tongue. We are not the only men who know of this paper.

When you ride to Bristol, not one of us must breathe a word of what we've found."

"Livesey," returned the squire, "you are always in the right of it. I'll be as silent as the grave."

Turn to page 10

With Treasure Island behind us, we were very short of men on board, so everyone had to lend a hand, save our wounded captain, who spent the days lying on a mattress and giving orders. We made a course for the nearest port in Spanish America, for we could not risk the voyage home without fresh hands.

It was just at sundown when we cast anchor in a most beautiful land-locked gulf, and were immediately surrounded by shore boats full of good local people selling fruits and vegetables. The joy on their good-humored faces, the taste of the tropical fruits, and above all the lights that began to shine in the town made a most charming contrast to our dark and bloody sojourn on the island.

The doctor, squire, and I went into town, and when we returned, Ben Gunn was on deck alone. He confessed that Silver was gone. Ben had allowed him to escape in a shore boat some hours ago, and he now assured us he had only done so to preserve our lives, which would certainly have been forfeit if "that man with the one leg had stayed aboard." The sea-cook had taken one of the sacks of coins with him, worth perhaps three or four hundred guineas, to help him on his further wanderings.

I think we were all pleased to be so cheaply rid of him.

To make a long story short, we got a few fresh hands on board, made a good cruise home, and the *Hispaniola* reached Bristol without any further drama. Five men only of those who had sailed returned with her. "Drink and the devil had done for the rest" with a vengeance.

All of us had an ample share of the treasure and used it wisely or foolishly, according to our natures. Captain Smollett is now retired from the sea. Gray not only saved his money, but also studied his profession, and he is now mate and part owner of a fine full-rigged ship, married, and the father of a family. As for Ben Gunn, he got a thousand pounds, which he spent or lost in three weeks, and was now begging.

Of Silver we have heard no more. That formidable seafaring man with one leg has at last gone clean out of my life; but I dare say he met his old wife, and perhaps still lives in comfort with her and Captain Flint (the parrot). At least, I hope so, for his chances of comfort in another world are very small.

We only took the gold, you know. The rest of the treasure remains where Flint buried it, and I certainly won't be going back to that accursed island, not even for such treasure. The worst dreams that ever I have are when I hear the surf booming about its coasts or start upright in bed with the sharp voice of Captain Flint still ringing in my ears: "Pieces of eight! Pieces of eight!"

THE END

I considered Captain Eaglehorn's offer, and then I answered. "I believe I've had enough adventure to last me quite some time. I nearly died in that apple barrel, and I don't wish to rush into danger again. I wish you the best of luck on your voyage, sir, but I would like swift passage to the nearest port."

"That would be Boston," the captain said as he rose, adjusting his uniform. "From there you can book passage home or wherever you're going. We will make way there with haste, young Jim."

The captain was true to his word. We sailed as though Captain Flint himself were hunting us, even navigating by starlight, splitting the crew in half for day and night sailing. My heart leaped when late one night I heard "Land ho!" I rushed to the bow and saw lights twinkling in the distance. I had never seen so many lanterns as in the port of Boston. The *Virtue* dropped anchor, and we waited for dawn to enter the city.

The port of Boston was busy and bustling. I stepped off the *Virtue*'s dinghy and onto the dock, amazed at the odd assortment of denizens. I heard a number of strange accents from the hands that moved about. When I returned from my trance, I realized that I was now alone in the new world, without a guardian or a cent to my name. That was certainly something I should have considered before departing. I had no coin to book passage home.

I would have to earn it. I could stay at the docks and see if I could find work. There was certainly enough labor to go around, judging by the perspiration on the brows of the dockhands. I could also venture into the city and see if I could find a trade that did not require me to return to sea.

If you would explore the city,
turn to page 41

If you would stay in port,
turn to page 72

The next morning, the pirates lit a fire fit to roast an ox that grew so hot, they could only approach it with great precaution from the windward side. In the same wasteful spirit, they cooked three times more than we could eat, and one of them, with an empty laugh, threw what was left into the fire, which blazed and roared again over this unusual fuel. I never in my life saw men so careless of tomorrow; surely they thought their lives might end this day, for today we would seek the treasure and encounter violence in so doing.

We made a curious figure as we set out to follow Flint's chart—all in soiled sailor clothes and all but me armed to the teeth. Silver had two guns slung about him, a great cutlass at his waist, and a pistol in each pocket of his square-tailed coat. His parrot perched upon his shoulder and gabbled odds and ends of purposeless sea-talk. I had a line about my waist and followed obediently after the sea-cook, who held the loose end of the rope, sometimes in his free hand, sometimes between his powerful teeth. For all the world, I was led like a dancing bear.

The other men were variously burdened with picks and shovels for treasure digging, and ample provisions for midday meal, and all with many weapons. Thus equipped, we set out—even the fellow with the broken head. As we walked, we regarded the instructions written on the chart near the big red cross:

> *Tall tree, Spy-glass shoulder,*
> *bearing a point to the N. of N.N.E.*
> *Skeleton Island E.S.E. and by E.*
> *Ten feet.*

A tall tree was thus the principal mark, but at a distance we could see the grove at the red cross was dotted with tall pine trees that rose above their neighbors, and it was impossible to discern to which tall tree Captain Flint referred without standing among them and using the compass.

When we arrived, I saw that this was a most pleasant portion of the island. Thickets of green nutmeg-trees were dotted here and there with the red columns and the broad shadow of the pines; and the first mingled their spice with the aroma of the others. The air, besides, was fresh and stirring, and this, under the sheer sunbeams, was a wonderful refreshment to our senses.

The party spread itself abroad, in a fan shape, shouting and leaping to and fro. We thus proceeded for about half a mile and were approaching the brow of the plateau when the man upon the farthest left began to cry aloud, as if in terror. Shout after shout came from him, and the others began to run in his direction.

"He can't 'a found the treasure," said old Morgan, hurrying past us from the right.

Indeed, as we found when we also reached the spot, it was something very different. At the foot of a pretty big pine and involved in a green creeper, which had even partly lifted some of the smaller bones, a human skeleton lay, with a few shreds of clothing, on the ground. I believe a chill struck for a moment to every heart.

"He was a seaman," said George Merry, who, bolder than the rest, had gone up close and was examining the rags of clothing. "Leastways, this is good sea-cloth."

"Aye, aye," said Silver; "you wouldn't look to find a bishop here, I reckon. But what sort of a way is that for bones to lie? 'Tain't in nature."

The skeleton had been posed and laid perfectly straight, his hands raised above his head pointing in a single direction.

"My old numbskull's got an idea," said Silver. "Here's the compass. Take a bearing along the line of them bones."

It was done. The body pointed straight in the direction Flint had written—E.S.E. by E.

"I thought so," cried the cook; "these bones are our pointer. Right up there are the jolly dollars! This is one of Flint's *jokes*.

He brought six men onto the island to hide the treasure, and he killed every one of them. He hauled this one here and laid him down by compass, shiver my timbers! If Flint were still alive, this would be a bad place for the lot of us."

"I saw Flint dead with these here deadlights," said Morgan. "And I ain't afraid of no ghosts."

"Dead—aye, sure enough he's dead and gone below," said the fellow with the bandage; "but if ever a spirit walked, it would be Flint's. Dear heart, but he died bad, did Flint."

"Aye, that he did," observed another.

"Come, come," said Silver; "stow this talk. He's dead, and he don't walk, that I know. Now let's move and find those doubloons."

We started up the hill; the pirates kept side by side and spoke with bated breath. The terror of the dead buccaneer had fallen on their spirits.

All of a sudden, out of the middle of the trees in front of us, a thin, high, trembling voice struck up the well-known air and words:

"Fifteen men on the dead man's chest—
Yo-ho-ho, and a bottle of rum!"

I never have seen men more dreadfully affected than the pirates. The color went from their six faces like enchantment; some leaped into the air, some clawed hold of others; Morgan groveled on the ground.

"It's Flint!" cried Merry.

The song stopped as suddenly as it began—broken off, you would have said, in the middle of a note, as though someone had laid his hand upon the singer's mouth. Coming through the clear, sunny atmosphere among the green treetops, I thought it had sounded airy and sweet; and the effect on my companions was the stranger.

While they cowered, I realized that none was observing me. In the confusion, I could slip the line about me and follow after the voice. Perhaps it was Dr. Livesey and the others playing a cruel joke on these cowardly cutthroats. But what if they caught me trying to escape? The pirates might kill me in their fear and anger.

If you would investigate the ghostly voice, turn to page 105

If you would encourage the pirates to keep moving, turn to page 99

*T*he council of buccaneers had lasted nearly an hour when the door opened and the five men, standing huddled together just inside, pushed one of their number forward. In any other circumstances it would have been comical to see his slow advance, hesitating as he set down each foot, but holding his closed right hand in front of him.

"Step up, lad," cried Silver. "I won't eat you. Hand it over, lubber."

Thus encouraged, the buccaneer stepped forth more briskly and handed something to Silver. The sea-cook looked at what had been given him.

"The black spot! I thought so," he observed. "I'm to be deposed as captain, then? But look here, now. You've cut this paper out of a Bible. What fool cuts a Bible? You're all doomed to misfortune."

This sent a ripple of uncertainty through their number, but then George, one of the remaining pirates, snapped. "Belay that talk, John Silver. The crew has spoken. You're out. Now come on. We're going to vote on a new captain."

"All right, then," said John Silver. "Vote! To begin, I nominate myself."

"You?" asked George. "You've just been deposed. Why would we vote for you?"

"Because I have this!" Silver cast down upon the floor a paper that I instantly recognized—none other than the chart on yellow paper, with the three red crosses, that I had found in the oilcloth at the bottom of the captain's chest. Why the doctor had given it to him was more than I could fancy.

The surviving mutineers leaped upon it like cats upon a mouse. It went from hand to hand, one tearing it from another; and by the oaths and the cries and the childish laughter with which they accompanied their examination, you would have thought they were already safe at home, counting their gold.

"It's really Flint's map," said one of their number. "I recognize the handwriting, and the way he ever did sign his name."

"So now who do you all support for captain?" asked Long John.

"Silver!" they cried. "Barbecue forever! Barbecue for cap'n!"

That was the end of the night's business, but it was long

before I could close an eye. My mind was full of thoughts of the events that had transpired on the island, and most of all I considered the remarkable game that Silver was playing—keeping the mutineers together with one hand and grasping with the other after every means, possible and impossible, to make his peace and save his miserable life.

Turn to page 25

"**H**elp you?" I asked. "You want me to save your neck, after all the evil deeds you've done?"

At the very least, Long John Silver appeared surprised by my response.

I said, "I told the captain and the others everything I heard in the apple barrel. I was the one who exposed your treachery. I was the one who let them onto you, so that they were prepared. Your men are dead because of me, Long John Silver, and I'll be overjoyed to watch you swing in Bristol, should I be lucky enough to live to see the day."

"I pray you do live to see it, Jim," the old pirate said drearily.

Turn to page 30

*L*ong John Silver wanted me to take a guess as to how the first mate, Mr. Arrow, met his demise, but I had long since made up my mind about the poor wretch's outcome.

"It all makes sense to me, lads," said I, hopping up on the table. Bowls of stew scattered, and the sailors howled. "Mr. Arrow was acting so peculiar because he was bewitched by the spell of a mermaid wizard under the sea!"

The crowd stared at me in stunned silence. I couldn't help it if their naivete prevented them from believing the truth.

"Don't you see? The mermaids disoriented him and made him intolerable, so that when he needed us most we would disregard him. He must have gone on deck late one night under the bright moon, and while he was up there he heard the mournful cries of the merfolk.

"Cries of the *what*?" asked Job Anderson, waving his cutlery at me. "I've got my fork right here!"

The others howled in amusement, slapping their thighs

and the table and banging their stew bowls. Food flew out of their mouths as they laughed.

"Oh sure, go on, laugh!" I hopped off the table and folded my arms defiantly. "But you won't be laughing when the mermaids set their sights on you. You'll be seduced the same as Mr. Arrow, and once those scaly, finned creatures of the sea cast a spell on you, you'll fall overboard as well, and if you're not drowned at once, you'll be pulled to their undersea kingdom, where you'll never see your families or friends or dry land ever again!"

As passionate as my speech was, the men returned to me nothing but hideous laughter. Some wiped tears and blew their noses, they were cackling so hard. But for all of their mockery, I knew for certain, deep down, that mermaids were part of our world.

Turn to page 136

"All right, then, Mr. Silver," I conceded. "It's not like I can refuse you. If I do, you'll open my gullet or stuff me in an ale barrel or some other such brutality, am I right?"

"Oh quite right," Long John admitted. "I can be quite murderous if it strikes my fancy."

I attempted to sneer like a pirate, and steeled myself for the mayhem ahead. I felt a rock in my stomach when I thought about the inevitable betrayal of my friends, but Silver was right. The map was his. And I remembered the smug laugh the squire and doctor had shared when I had found it and they first realized where it led. I had waltzed right into their supper and gifted them a pirate king's buried treasure. They wouldn't be laughing in the end.

Long John Silver instructed me to say nothing of Black Dog, and to go about my business as if I were still an ally of the squire and doctor.

That afternoon I toured the vessel with my former friends,

and learned that the captain was a stiff man named Smollett who suspected mutiny. I nearly blanched, for I was surprised to learn that the moral souls aboard were already onto us.

The next night, under sail and under stars, I confronted Long John Silver by one of the apple barrels. "What exactly is our plan? The captain is a sharp fellow. He already suspects an insurrection."

"At ease, Jimmy, at ease." Long John Silver patted me on the head as he balanced on his crutch. There'll be no mutiny before we reach Treasure Island. We need your friends to strain their backs hauling the riches for us, and we need your dear, suspicious captain to set a course away from the island. Once our return journey is underway, then we will strike, and we'll keel-haul the lubbers for the fun of it."

"What's this now?" came a voice, and a loud crunch, as the first mate, Mr. Arrow, approached and bit into a plump, ripe apple that he held in one hand. Mr. Arrow was a brown old sailor with earrings in his ears and a squint. He chewed noisily on the apple, his other hand on his hip—where an armed pistol was braced.

"Get outta here, you old drunk," spat Silver, swatting at Arrow with his crutch. "I wouldn't've recommended you for this voyage if you were worth your weight in sea-water."

"I have found my first mate to be quite resourceful in spite of his foibles," replied another voice. Captain Smollett came upon Silver and me from the other side, flanked by Livesey and

Trelawney. The look on their faces was that of disappointment and betrayal. They all had pistols trained on us.

"How could you, Jim?" asked Dr. Livesey.

"I'll have you in irons," the captain told Long John. "Now talk—who else among the crew is your co-conspirator?"

By dawn, every pirate aboard our schooner was rounded up and chained. I feared the captain would make us walk the plank, but he was not barbaric as all that. We returned to England, where all but I was forced to stand trial and were hung. I was sent on a coach back to the Admiral Benbow inn, penniless and shamed. Trelawney and Livesey never returned. Some say they retired to London in great wealth, while my only reward was learning the fate of immoral pirates.

THE END

"**S**tay your hand, sir!" I cried, leaping in front of the captain's blade.

"Jim, no!" Dr. Livesey exclaimed, breaking his casual posture. "This matter is between one man and one fool, and does not involve you, manly and foolish though you are." When the doctor spoke, it was often hard to tell if he was complimenting or scolding. But either way, he did not want me to get involved. I eyed the captain's knife, gleaming like a murderous star. It seemed that like it or not, I now was very much involved.

I had played at fighting as a young child, but had no real training to prepare me to truly be of much help. But I did my best to stand my ground.

"This matter does not concern you, boy!" The captain snarled, "Stand aside, or you and your powdery friend will be two morsels of meat on a single skewer."

"Pay the boy no mind," Dr. Livesey told the captain.

"Your quarrel is with me."

"Aye, that it is," the captain said, meeting the doctor's gaze. I feared that blood would be shed in the very next moment.

Turn to page 116

After my painful struggle in the apple barrel, I was determined not to return to sea so soon, and so I set out to explore the city of Boston. In the Common I heard news that a silversmith of some renown was looking for a new apprentice, so I set out for his shop, hoping to learn a new trade and earn money for passage home.

When I arrived, the strong smell of the workshop's vapors burned my nose. Acrid smoke billowed out of the chimney and the open windows. Inside, it was dreadfully hot, and I called out to the man in the thick apron hammering over the anvil, which made such cacophonous noise, I had to shout and cover my ears.

Turning away from his work, the silversmith narrowed his eyes at me, but when he realized I was there about the apprenticeship, he nodded and waved me out into the yard.

"Have an interest in metalwork, do you, boy? Well, I'd be willing to take you on. But I hope you're the cautious sort. My last apprentice was a boy named Johnny who spilled molten silver on his fingers and fused them all together! Could've cost the boy his hand, or even his life. I hope nothing of that sort happens to you, eh, boy?"

"Certainly, I hope not, sir."

"All right, good." The silversmith grabbed me by the collar and pulled me around to the side of his workshop, where not a single person from the street could see or hear us. "Now let me tell you one other thing. If you work for me, you're going to be running messages for the resistance, got it? We're no fans of Georgie here in Massachusetts. So get comfortable, lad, because you're going to help my friends and me declare our independence from His Majesty."

"All right, good sir. I will aid you on your quest for independence. But . . . what is your name, sir?"

"Me?" He flashed a wide and toothy smile. You can call me Paul Revere."

THE END

I think if I had been able, that I would have killed him through the barrel, but I knew that to flee now would almost certainly mean being caught. Meantime, Long John ran on, little supposing he was overheard.

"Here it is about gentlemen of fortune. They live rough lives, and they risk the hangman's noose, but they eat and drink like fighting-cocks, and when a cruise is done, why, it's hundreds of pounds instead of hundreds of farthings in their pockets. Now, the most goes for rum and merrymaking, and then back to sea they go with not a pence to show for it, but that's not the course I lay. I puts it all away, some here, some there, and none too much anywhere, by reason of suspicion. I'm fifty, mark you; once I'm back from this cruise, I'll set up as an earnest gentleman in earnest. Maybe you think it's about time. Ah, but I've lived easy in the meantime, never denied myself anything my heart desires, and slep' soft and ate dainty all my days but when at sea.

And how did I begin? Before the mast, like you!"

"Well," said the other, "but all the other money's gone now, ain't it? You daren't show face in Bristol after this."

"Why, where might you suppose it was?" asked Silver derisively.

"At Bristol, in banks and places," answered his companion.

"It were," said the cook; "it were when we weighed anchor. But my old missis has it all by now. And the Spy-glass is sold, lease and goodwill and rigging; and the old girl's off to meet me. I would tell you where, for I trust you, but it'd make jealousy among the mates."

"And can you trust your missis?" asked the other.

"Gentlemen of fortune," returned the cook, "usually trusts little among themselves, and right they are, you can bet on it. But I have a way with me, I have. There was some that was feared of Pew, and some that was feared of Flint; but Flint his own self was feared of me. Feared he was, and proud. None dare cross Long John Silver."

"Well, I tell you now," replied the lad, "I didn't half a quarter like the job till I had this talk with you, John; but there's my hand on it now."

"And a brave lad you were, and smart, too," answered Silver, shaking hands so heartily that the apple barrel shook. "A finer figurehead for a gentleman of fortune I never clapped my eyes on."

By this time I had begun to understand the meaning of

their terms. By a "gentleman of fortune" they plainly meant neither more nor less than a common pirate, and the little scene that I had overheard was the last act in the corruption of one of the honest hands—perhaps of the last one left aboard. But on this point I was soon to be relieved, for upon Silver giving a little whistle, a third man strolled up and sat down by the party.

"Dick's square," said Silver.

"Oh, I know'd Dick was square," returned the voice of the coxswain, Israel Hands. "He's no fool, is Dick." He spat. "But look here," he went on, "here's what I want to know, Barbecue: How long are we a-going to stand off and on like a blessed bumboat? I've had a'most enough o' Cap'n Smollett; he's hazed me long enough, by thunder! I want to go into that cabin, I do. I want their pickles and wines, and that."

"Israel," said Silver, "your head ain't good for much, nor ever was. But you can hear, I reckon; at least, your ears is big enough. Now, here's what I say: You'll berth forward, and you'll live hard, and you'll speak soft, and you'll keep sober till I give the word."

"But when? When do we strike?" growled the coxswain.

"When! By the powers!" cried Silver. "Well now, if you want to know, I'll tell you when. The last moment I can manage, and that's when. Here's a first-rate seaman, Cap'n Smollett, sails the blessed ship for us. Here's this squire and doctor with a map and such. I don't know where it is, do I? No more do you, says you. Well then, I mean this squire and doctor shall find the stuff, and help us to get it aboard, by the powers. Then we'll see. If I was sure of you all, sons of double Dutchmen, I'd have Cap'n Smollett navigate us half-way back again before I struck."

"Why, we're all seamen aboard here, I should think," said the lad Dick.

"We're all forecastle hands, you mean," snapped Silver. We can steer a course, but who's to set one? We need the cap'n, at least till he works us back into the trades."

"But," asked Dick, "when we do lay 'em athwart, what are we to do with 'em, anyhow?"

"There's the man for me!" cried the cook admiringly. "That's what I call business. Well, what would you think? Put 'em ashore like maroons? That would have been England's way. Or cut 'em down like that much pork? That would have been Flint's, or Billy Bones's."

Israel smiled. "Billy always said, 'Dead men don't bite.' Well, he's dead now hisself."

"Wise words," said Silver. "I vote for killing them all. When I'm back home and rich, I don't want none of these sea-lawyers in the cabin a-coming home after some miraculous rescue. Wait until the time comes, I say; but when it comes, slit their throats. Oh! And I claim Trelawney. I'll wring his calf's head off his body with these hands." Suddenly he broke off. "Dick! Fetch me an apple. I want to wet my pipe."

You may fancy the terror I was in! I could hear the lad's footsteps creaking on the deck. It was now or never. If I ran, they would almost certainly spot me, but if I stayed in the apple barrel where I was, save some divine intervention, I would very likely be found.

What was I to do?

If you would stay put,
turn to page 161

If you would run for it,
turn to page 81

All hands were already congregated at the bow; many stared into the distance at the land that had just been sighted. A belt of fog had lifted almost simultaneously with the appearance of the moon. Away to the southwest of us we saw two low hills, a couple of miles apart, and rising behind one of them a third and higher hill, whose peak was still buried in the fog. All three seemed sharp and conical in figure.

It all seemed like a dream to me, for I had not yet recovered from my horrid fear of a minute or two before. Then I heard the voice of Captain Smollett issuing orders to sail the *Hispaniola* on a course clear of the island to the east.

"And now, men," said the captain, when the sails were fixed, "has any one of you ever seen that land ahead?"

"I have, sir," said Silver. "I've watered there with a trader I was cook in. Skeleton Island, they calls it. It were a main place for pirates once. That hill to the north they call Fore-mast Hill; and then the three hills run southward—fore, main, and mizzen, sir. But the main—that's the big un, with the cloud on it—they usually calls the Spy-glass, by reason of a lookout they kept there when they cleaned their ships, sir."

"I have a chart here," says the captain. "See if that's the place."

Long John's eyes burned in his head as he took the chart, but by the fresh look of the paper, I knew he was doomed to disappointment. This was not the map I found in Billy Bones's chest, but an accurate copy, complete in all things—names and heights and soundings—with the single exception of the red crosses and the written notes. He must have been so annoyed, but Silver had the strength of mind to hide it.

"Yes, sir," said he, "this is the spot, to be sure."

"Thank you," said Captain Smollett. "You may go."

I was surprised at the coolness with which John avowed his knowledge of the island. In contrast, I was half-frightened when he drew near to me. He did not know I had overheard his council from the apple barrel, but I was terribly horrified by his cruelty, duplicity, and power that I could scarce conceal a shudder when he laid his hand upon my arm.

"Ah," said he, "this here is a sweet spot, this island—a sweet spot for a lad to get ashore on. You'll bathe, and you'll climb trees and hunt goats, you will. It's a pleasant thing to be young and have ten toes. I miss it. When you want to go exploring, you just ask old John, and he'll put up a snack for you to take along."

And clapping me in the friendliest way upon the shoulder, he hobbled off forward and went below.

Turn to page 145

"Jim, don't be foolish!" the doctor pleaded, but I had made up my mind. I was not going to let those mutinous pirates murder one of our party and get away with it. Looking back, Redruth died because of the map that I had found. The guilt of responsibility weighed heavy on my heart, as heavy as the pistol that Joyce placed in my hand.

The captain and squire shouted oaths at me and told me what a reckless fool I was, and I couldn't help but smile because the captain and squire finally agreed on something. Joyce and I moved quickly down the knoll, arms at the ready, until the sounds of our friends' pleas had faded.

"It's hard to see," Joyce said, peering between the thick trees that were suddenly all around us. "Those scurvy dogs must be here somewhere."

But my keen young eyes could see them.

It was probably better that he couldn't see them because he would have known greater terror than he already felt. I myself was breathing heavily and thinking back on my childhood at the Inn. I wondered to myself if my mother would ever hear of my adventures.

The pirates had us surrounded, weapons trained. I heard the crack of firing muskets, and nothing more.

THE END

It was unwise to venture down into the woods—that much was clear. I was dead tired, as well, and likely to make poor judgments if I didn't get some rest. After hearing that there had been a mutiny after I'd left the ship, we all chose to stay in the log-house and not risk our lives further tonight. When I got to sleep, which was not till after a great deal of tossing, I slept like a log of wood.

The others had long been up and had already breakfasted when I was wakened by a bustle and the sound of voices.

"Flag of truce!" I heard someone say. "And carried by Silver himself!"

I jumped up, rubbing my eyes, and ran to a loophole in the wall. It was quite early, and the coldest morning that I think I ever experienced in my time abroad—it chilled me to the marrow. The sky was bright and cloudless, but there was Silver, knee-deep in low white vapor that had crawled during the night out of the morass.

"Keep indoors, men," said the captain. "Ten to one this is a trick."

Then he hailed the buccaneer.

"Who goes? Stand, or we fire."

"Flag of truce," cried Silver. "I've come to discuss terms."

"Have it out, then," said the captain.

Silver had terrible hard work getting up the knoll, but he stayed focused and at last arrived at the log-house door.

"Sit down," said the captain. "We're not letting you inside. You said truce. So talk. Let's hear terms."

"As you like," said the sea-cook. "We want the treasure, and we'll have it. I reckon you prefer your lives to treasure. So give us the chart to go get the treasure, and we'll offer you a choice. Either you come aboard with us, and once the treasure is shipped, on my honor I'll leave you somewhere safe ashore. Or if you prefer, you can stay here. We'll divide stores with you, and I'll send the first ship we meet here to pick you up."

"Is that all?" Captain Smollett asked as he rose to his full height.

"Every last word, by thunder!" answered John. "Refuse that, and you've seen the last of me but musket-balls."

"Very good," said the captain. "Now here is my proposal. Come up here one by one, unarmed, and I'll clap you all in irons and take you home for a fair trial in England. If you won't, I'll see you all to Davy Jones. You can't find the treasure without us. You can't sail the ship without us. So you can't fight us. So surrender. These are the last kind words you'll get from me, Long John Silver. I'll put a bullet in your back when next I meet you."

Silver struggled to his feet. "I'll kill every last one of you. You'll feel swords in your bellies before the day is done." And with a dreadful oath he stumbled off.

"Stations! To your stations!" called the captain, and we all rushed to our loopholes to prepare for an assault. There was a round score of muskets for the seven of us; the firewood had been built into four piles—tables, you might say—and ammunition was laid out on each of these. In the middle, the cutlasses lay ranged.

"Jim, come here," the doctor said. "The fighting will start soon, and you mustn't die needlessly. You're no help to us here."

"I can fight, sir," said I. "I can and I will."

"Fine, but you should try to live. Go into the jungle. Gather supplies and fresh food if you can find it. Stay clear until you hear no more sounds of muskets and steel."

Could I really go? Could I leave my friends behind to their fate? What kind of mate would I be if I abandoned them at this critical moment? But then again, if I left, when the fighting was done, I could return fresh. Perhaps I could help treat the wounded or cause a diversion at a critical juncture. What was I to do?

If you would leave to gather supplies,
turn to page 125

If you would stay with your friends,
turn to page 141

urely Captain Eaglehorn thought me mad, to consider for even one instant staying aboard a vessel on the high seas after the ordeal I had overcome in the apple barrel, but I had left my home and gone to sea to have an island adventure, and I would not let Long John Silver and those other mutinous dogs deny me that experience and glory. I told the captain that I would stay with his crew on the *Virtue*, in any role he would have me. I would earn my keep, doing all I could to help make his voyage a success.

The captain nodded and clapped me on the shoulder, saying that he thought he saw the mark of the sea on me. The crew made me feel at home, introducing themselves and offering me space and fresh clothes and rations. I met some of the passengers aboard, who, like Squire Trelawney, had financed the expedition. They included Bart Snidley, a director of theater out of New York who assured me he was quite famous in the colonies, and an actress named Fay who had platinum tresses and an ever-changing wardrobe. There was also a man named Alligator Stevens, who introduced himself as a wilderness guide. He always hung about the deck, squinting his eyes in the sun but never shading them, chewing on a pipe, and practicing his knots on a length of rope.

The weeks were quiet and the weather fair, and we found a current to take us to their island destination. I often wondered what had happened to the *Hispaniola* and the innocent souls aboard. Captain Smollett had suspected danger, of course, and so must have taken precautions to avoid a deadly mutiny. Perhaps he had won the squire over to the side of reason, and they were able to resist the treachery.

Of course these thoughts could not do anything to improve the situation aboard the *Hispaniola*, for I was aboard the *Virtue*, a vessel of the New World destined for uncharted lands. When a voice from the crow's nest shouted "Land ho!" I leaped from my hammock excitedly. At last, at long last, we had found our island.

And what an island it was. Black clouds in the sky parted like Mr. Snidley's theater curtains, revealing a craggy island dominated by a large rounded mountain at its center, which loomed evilly like the severed head of a murderer whose sentence had been carried out. As the sun fled below the horizon, we could see torches lit in the small caves on the mountain's face, forming what looked like glowing red eyes, nose, and mouth. Indeed, the island as a whole resembled a skull boiled clean.

"At last!" cheered Bart Snidley, leaning over the port side railing and applauding with cupped hands. "I'll be sure to find curiosities for my next show now!"

"Curiosities?" I asked, feeling like whatever they were, Bart Snidley was one of them.

"Why, yes, my boy! Exotic fauna! Strange foods! All sorts of things to wonder and delight the audiences of His Majesty's colonies! That's why we're here, in an uncharted land, to capture and bring home wonders that will line our pockets with the hard-earned currency of ordinary people prepared to be marveled!"

The whole crew rushed the deck, eager to see the destination at the end of their long voyage. I saw so many expressions on their faces—relief and fear and excitement and greed and so much more. I saw a thirst for adventure, and trepidation about the unknown. The emotions were displayed clearly as the crew and passengers looked out at the island with the skull mountain at its center. I held my breath as we approached the island, for I knew not what I would find there.

As we approached the island, the sea had fallen into total darkness, and we lit lanterns to shine upon the water and find our way to the coast. Even so, we did not anticipate the jagged rocks that filled the cove like treacherous caltrops submerged below the water's surface. We were trapped. Leaks sprang and flooded the lower holds. As crewmen rushed to seal the leaks, we saw many men with spears rushing down the mountain towards the shore. They shouted war cries and pointed their weapons at us. I could understand their rage. We were alien savages who had come to their shore.

I braced myself for what was to come.

Turn to page 113

"Hello, little friend," I said, reaching out to pet the snake on its flat, scaly head. Little did I suppose that he was a deadly enemy and that the noise I had heard was the famous rattle.

The creature reared back and then struck out. I felt a slight pinch and looked down to see the snake's fangs embedded in my hand. I grabbed it and pulled it away, revealing two puncture wounds just beyond my knuckles. Feeling quite foolish, even more foolish because I could not move my fingers, and most foolish because I suddenly felt the distinct urge to sit down.

My arm was getting stiff, and I was sweating profusely. Though my vision blurred, I saw the snake slither away.

My lungs felt thick, and I struggled to breathe. I needed to lie down. As my head rested on the ground, never to rise again, I determined that, in fact, the snake was not very friendly after all.

THE END

In the darkness I found myself dreadfully turned around. As I walked across the island, I came upon where I thought I first met Ben Gunn, the maroon, and I continued past in what I supposed was the direction he had come from. Many wretched hours passed, and I might be stumbling in those dark woods still if I had not spotted a wavering glow against the sky, where, as I judged, Ben was cooking his supper before a roaring fire. And yet I wondered, in my heart, why he would show himself so careless, for if I could see this radiance, might it not reach the eyes of Silver himself where he camped upon the shore among the marshes?

I followed the glow until it was red and hot and clearly the embers of a smoldering bonfire. To my surprise, the fire burned outside my company's log-house! By this time, I had been away for many hours and was grateful to return and greet my friends. Inside, the darkness was absolute, and

I could distinguish nothing but the sounds of snoring and clacking. What was that clacking?

With my arms before me I walked stealthily in, but my foot struck something yielding—it was a sleeper's leg.

And then, all of a sudden, a shrill voice broke forth out of the darkness:

"Pieces of eight! Pieces of eight! Pieces of eight! Pieces of eight! Pieces of eight!" and so forth, without pause or change, like the clacking of a tiny mill.

It was Silver's green parrot, Captain Flint! It was she whom I had heard pecking. At her sharp, clipping tones, the sleepers awoke and sprang up. With a mighty oath, the voice of Silver cried, "Who goes?"

I turned to run but crashed full into the arms of two pirates, who held me tight.

"Bring a torch, Dick," said Silver when my capture was thus assured.

Dick left and returned shortly with a lighted brand. The red glow of the torch lit up the interior of the log-house, and my worst fears were realized. The pirates were in possession of the house and stores, and not a prisoner or friend in sight. I could only judge that all had perished.

There were six of the buccaneers, all told; not another man was left alive. Five were on their feet, but the sixth lay on his back in the corner, gravely wounded from the previous battle.

The parrot sat, preening her plumage, on Long John's shoulder. The man looked paler and more stern than normal, and worse for wear.

"So," said he, "here's Jim Hawkins, shiver my timbers! Dropped in, like, eh? Well, come, I take that friendly. Sit down, boys. Mr. Hawkins will forgive your lack of courtesy."

The pirates set me with my back against the wall, and I stood there, looking Silver in the face, with black despair in my heart.

Silver sighed. "Jim, Jim, Jim. I've always liked you. You remind me of myself when I was young and handsome. I always wanted you to join us and take your share, you know? But you had to go and wander off away from your captain and squire and doctor and all them. Now they're dead set against you. 'Duty is duty, and that Hawkins abandoned his post,' said the captain, last I spoke to him."

My friends, then, were still alive. I partly believed Silver's statement that they were incensed that I had deserted my post, but I was more relieved to learn that while the pirates now occupied the stockade, the others were not dead.

"Why are you here?" I asked. "And where are my friends?"

"Wouldn't you like to know!" sneered one of the pirates.

"Now, now," Silver soothed, "let's show Mr. Hawkins some respect. You see, Jim, Dr. Livesey came down with a flag of truce. He offered us everything: supplies, the stockade, even the *Hispaniola* herself. All they wanted was freedom to leave the log-house untouched, and so they were obliged. I honestly don't know where they've gone."

He took a deep breath. "And, Jim, I'm sorry to say, but they didn't have a kind word to say about you. Didn't even count you among their number when I asked."

"Is that all?" I asked.

"Well, it's all that you're to hear, my son," returned Silver.

"And now I am to choose?"

"You can join us if you wish," returned Silver.

"I say we kill him now," said Morgan, one of the pirates I had met that first day in Long John's public-house. He sprang up, drawing his knife and moving towards me.

"Avast, there!" cried Silver. "Maybe you thought you were the captain, Tom Morgan, but I'll teach you better."

"I think Morgan is right," said one of the other pirates.

"Aye," said another. "I'm sick of you protecting this miserable rat, John Silver. We could all hang because of this boy."

Silver roared, "You want to have it out with *me*? Have at me, then, you gentlemen o' fortune. Take a cutlass, him that dares, and I'll see the color of his insides, crutch and all."

Not a man stirred; not a man answered.

"That's what I thought," Long John added.

Then Morgan finally spoke. "This crew has rights, Cap'n Silver. We'll have a council. Outside, men, follow me."

And so with one remark or another all marched out and left Silver and me alone with the torch.

"Now, look you here, Jim Hawkins," Silver said in a steady whisper, "you're within half a plank of death and torture. I've stood by you through thick and thin. Now I'll keep these common cutthroats from killing you, but when the time comes, you must save Long John from swinging. Understand?"

If you would promise to protect Long John Silver, turn to page 85

If you would refuse, turn to page 33

It was too dangerous to go ashore. Without any adults to protect me, Long John Silver or one of the other pirates would have complete freedom to slit my throat at their convenience. Better to stay with my own people.

The doctor and I watched the men as they landed on the beach, lashed their boats to trees, and tromped off beyond the tree line, though they left a man behind to guard each boat. The pirates who remained aboard the *Hispaniola* were similarly idle and irritable.

"Come, Jim," the doctor whispered, leading me over to the jolly-boat. "Do you remember that stockade upon the map? Let's grab Hunter and scout up there for information."

I thought this was a fine plan, and so I joined the two men in the little boat. We rowed to the coast and around, to find a clearer path to the top of the knoll where the stockade was marked.

As we disembarked, I watched Dr. Livesey make ready.

He wore a big silk handkerchief under his hat for coolness's sake and a brace of pistols ready primed for safety.

A hundred yards up from the beach, we reached the stockade. A spring of clear water rose almost at the top of the knoll. On the knoll, and enclosing the spring, they had built a stout log-house fit to hold two score of people in a pinch and loopholed for musketry on either side. Inside, the space was wide and clear, and the place was so secure that anyone defending the log-house could do so against a regiment.

"This is the place where we will make our stand against the pirates," the doctor said. "Things are well enough in the cabin of the *Hispaniola*, with arms and food, but here there is fresh water. If the pirates can't find any, they will be forced to face us when we have the high ground."

Worried for our friends still on the schooner, we made water fly, and soon we were back aboard the *Hispaniola*. We told them the plan to take the stockade and settled on the details of its accomplishment.

Joyce and the doctor set to work loading the jolly-boat with provisions, while the captain and squire stayed on deck, approaching the coxswain and other scurvy dogs still aboard. Redruth circled behind the pirates, cutting off their retreat, and I watched from the side, though Squire Trelawney had forbidden me from doing so.

"Mr. Hands," the captain said, showing him that both

squire and captain had cocked pistols in each hand, "if any of you six make a signal of any description, we'll shoot you dead. Now get down in the galley and stay down, you dogs."

The pirates wisely obeyed. By this time, the doctor had the jolly-boat loaded as much as we dared. This second trip aroused the suspicion of the two guards that remained at the boats ashore, and one of them took off through the trees. We proceeded without pausing to take breath, till the whole of our cargo was delivered to the log-house.

With the doctor's permission, I had set out to scout the perimeter of the stockade to see if there were any gaps in our defenses, when I saw a strange man running up the hill towards me.

"Who are you?" I asked.

"Ben Gunn," he answered, and his voice sounded hoarse and awkward, like a rusty lock. "I'm poor Ben Gunn, I am; and I haven't spoke with a living soul these three years."

He was a man with pleasing features, though his skin, wherever it was exposed, was burnt by the sun. He was clothed with tatters of old ship's canvas and old sea-cloth, and this extraordinary patchwork was all held together by a system of the most various and incongruous fastenings: brass buttons, bits of stick, and loops of tarry gaskin. About his waist he wore an old brass-buckled leather belt, which was the one thing solid in his whole outfit.

"Three years!" I cried. "Were you shipwrecked?"

"Nay, mate," said he; "marooned with no one but some goats. What do you call yourself, mate?"

"Jim," I told him.

"Well, Jim, I now believe it were Providence that put me here, for I'll let you in on a secret. I'm rich!"

I now felt sure that the poor fellow had gone crazy in his solitude.

"Now, Jim, you tell me true: Is that Flint's crew in yonder stockade?" he asked.

At this I believed that I had found an ally, and I answered him at once.

"No, but some of Flint's old comrades are after us. We're here to defend ourselves."

I told him the whole story of our voyage and the predicament in which we found ourselves. He heard me with the keenest interest, and when I had finished, he moved to pat me on the top of the head.

"You're a good lad, Jim. Just put your trust in Ben Gunn— Ben Gunn's the man to do it. Would you think it likely, now, that your squire would prove a liberal-minded one in case of help?"

"He's right inside. You could come up with me and ask him."

"No, no, I couldn't possibly. But I was on Flint's ship when he buried the treasure here, and had three years stranded to explore, and I know a thing or two. Maybe I can help you later." And with a wink he ran down the hill, away from me.

A sudden tremendous explosion sounded, the cacophonous growl of a cannon firing, and then an assault of small arms. I hurried back to the log-house, but by the time I arrived, the shooting was done and the men were standing over the body of poor Redruth, one of our own. He was dead and gone.

"What happened?" I cried.

With an oath, the squire said, "The pirates assaulted us and caught our man. We took out a few of theirs, don't worry. Looks like they retreated into the wood."

"We should go after them," said Joyce, "and avenge poor Redruth."

"Nay," the captain replied. "It's too dangerous, and night is coming. We don't want to split our party or be caught unawares."

"Are you going to stand for that, Jim?" asked Joyce. "Come with me. I'll give you a brace of pistols, and we'll shoot those pirates dead, starting with Long John Silver."

If you would stay in the log-house,
turn to page 53

If you would go with Joyce,
turn to page 51

The port of Boston reminded me much of Bristol, and after my many adventures in search of Treasure Island, I did not desire to abandon the sea. What even would I do in the city? Work at an inn, as I had at the Admiral Benbow? It would not do. I could almost hear my mother's criticism. "Journey across the world to do just what you were doing at home?" I could not stomach it. I would stay close to the sea.

I walked past dock and domicile, searching for signs of wanted work.

"Looking for labor and a wage, lad?" asked a man with a high voice. He sat on a coil of heavy rope on the side of the road.

I said, "If both be fair, aye."

"They're quite fair, fair and extraordinary," said the stranger.

"Who are you?" I asked.

"Call me Ishmael," said he. "I want you to meet my captain."

As if summoned, I heard strange footsteps behind me. *Click, thud, click, thud, click, thud.* I turned and saw a commanding man before me. He had steely eyes and a harpoon in his hands, and where one of his legs should have been, a wooden peg leg was instead.

"I'm the captain," the steely eyed man said. "Now tell me, boy, what do you know about whales?"

I knew next to nothing, but I would learn, putting my trust in another seaman with only one leg. As part of his crew I would sail the ocean, and hunt whales, and have grand adventures, but that is a tale for another time.

THE END

I couldn't do it. As far as I could tell, the lady Fay was about to become a human sacrifice, and whatever fate was to befall me, it couldn't possibly be worse than that. I held my tongue as the woman was lashed to the wooden obelisk and dangled off the ledge of the cliff. My vision did not extend far beyond the cliff's edge, for the bright torches that lined the cliff created a near-impenetrable layer of darkness beyond, but there was something moving out there. I saw large dark shapes shift. And then without warning a hand reached out of the darkness. It was covered in fur, and if it were held flat, a foursome could easily have dined at a table on the outstretched palm. The hand closed around the woman and, with a snap, broke off the obelisk at its base. The hand retreated into the darkness, carrying the woman with it.

Our captors let out thunderous cheers at the spectacle. Their ululations continued for some time; they seemed pleased with the outcome of their ceremony—the giant hand, and whatever creature was attached to it, carrying the woman off into the darkness.

With the lashings tight around my wrists, my hands felt cold and numb, but as I started to drift into unconsciousness from exhaustion, we were suddenly moving again. They carried us along the cliff's edge, and then down another ridge, down the mountain, still in darkness. It was impossible to see where we were going. I could hear the others groan. We were all suffering.

At last they cut our bonds and we fell on our backs in the dirt. I could see that torches lit the whole area where they had taken us—we lay near a large pit dug out of the dirt, dotted with heavy shale rocks. It was ten feet deep and thirty feet square.

I could not move without our captors threatening me with spears. I watched as they cast two of our lot into the pit—Alligator Stevens and the cook, Stewbeef. The cook's big potbelly and the guide's glistening muscles could not have contrasted more. Our captors tossed a pair of knives into the pit, one at the feet of each man. The two of them looked at each other, horrified, then down at the blades. They tried to rush for the edges of the pit, but they were menaced with spears when they tried to climb out of the slippery pit, so they turned to face each other, resigned to their unjust fate. I closed my eyes, unable to watch, but still I could hear the carnage.

When at last the crowd let out one final cheer, I opened my eyes and they were pulling Alligator Stevens victorious from the pit, and also the blood-drenched body of the cook. Before I could truly react, I was rolled into the bloodstained pit myself. I landed face-first. Pain shot through my hands and knees. I ached. I was tired.

I heard a howl of pain and looked to see Captain Eaglehorn down in the pit with me. "It's all right, boy," he told me as he rose to his feet. "Just stay still, and I promise I'll get this over with just as quickly as I am able."

He reached for one of the knives and rushed at me, but I was more nimble than he and managed to shuffle around the pit's perimeter, keeping clear of his reach to avoid his strikes. In frustration, he threw the knife, but it narrowly missed me. I tried to crawl past him to escape, but he grabbed at me, and I had no choice but to roll against him to break his grip. He toppled over, striking his head on the ground.

"Finish it, boy. Hurry!" The voice came from the edge of the pit above me. It was Alligator Stevens. "Do you want to live, or don't you?"

There was a rock close by, a heavy stone. With that rock I could end this. But I couldn't. Could I?

"Go on," said the captain. "What are you waiting for?"

If you would kill the captain,
turn to page 176

If you would spare the captain,
turn to page 119

My mother had seen hardship in her life, and it had awarded her no small amount of guts and stubbornness, but now was no time for such qualities, in the face of coin-hungry buccaneers bearing down on our inn and home.

"Mother, mother, please!" I implored her. "The captain's unfulfilled tab will not bankrupt us. We mustn't wager our lives for a few coins. Let those salty men have the sea-chest and depart. It will all be over soon, and we can go on as before."

It makes me blush to admit that I brought tears to Mother's eye with that speech, for she touched my hair and confessed her pride in raising such a handsome and reasonable young man. She agreed to stay in the hamlet until the danger had passed.

Unsurprisingly, the charity of the hamlet's denizens returned once a contribution did not include facing down a band of vicious pirates. We had no trouble finding a place to stay the night while we waited for the storm of pirates to pass. By morning, the coast was clear, cloudless and pirate-less; mother and I returned to the Admiral Benbow to inspect the damage.

The front door had been broken off its hinges, but fortunately the wood was still intact. It could be repaired with minor handiwork. The bottles of our finest spirits had been drained or removed entirely. As I climbed the stairs to the captain's room, I feared what I would find.

It was eerily quiet as I climbed the stairs. I had no expectation that I would encounter anyone but I slowed my steps to be sure and listened closely before entering the captain's quarters. There was no one there.

The sea-chest was gone, and the rest of the place was ransacked. Feathers were everywhere, for even the mattress and cushions of the bed had been sliced open and their contents spread liberally about the room. On the windowsill, I found a single item untouched—the captain's old spy-glass.

In the decades that followed, it became apparent that the excitement and adventure of my life had been unevenly distributed, concentrated in my early years. Things were peaceful at the Admiral Benbow after that fateful night. Mother passed ownership of the inn to me when I came of age, and I served as a fair keeper of the place. To this day, on clear mornings I walk out to the cliffs and gaze across the sea with the captain's spy-glass, which I have kept all these years. Sometimes when the wind blows I can almost hear the captain's old sea shanty, *Yo-ho-ho and a bottle of rum,* and I wonder how my life would have been different if I had gotten my hands on the pirate captain's sea-chest. It might have led me on a great adventure.

THE END

s the boy, Dick, approached the apple barrel where I was hiding, I knew my time was short; I had to act or I would soon be found, and for all I knew Long John Silver and the other pirates would promptly relieve my body of its head. I had to run for it, even if the risk was great.

With a tremendous burst of strength and speed, I leaped from the apple barrel and landed on the deck, silent, like a cat on the prowl. To my surprise, the others were all facing my direction. At the very least, they seemed just as surprised as I, if not more so.

"Jim!" the cook said, his gaze narrowing. "What were you doing in that apple barrel?"

"Looking for an apple to eat, sir."

"But there are no apples in that apple barrel, Jim."

"That's true." I scratched the back of my head nervously. "I believe I fell asleep, sir."

"In the apple barrel?" he asked, sounding incredulous.

"Yes, sir. It was the lull of the ocean waves, I'd wager, knocked me right out."

He hissed an angry oath. "Who falls asleep in an apple barrel? That's the most ridic'lous lie I ever heard told, Jim Hawkins. Now answer me true—how much did you hear of my conversation with Master Hands and young Dick here?"

"I heard enough, Long John Silver." I tried to keep my speech brave, as I knew my death was as close as the distance across the deck between these ragged buccaneers and me.

"Enough to know that I sailed with Captain Flint?" asked Silver. The look on my face must have given him the answer he sought, for he immediately added, "And I suppose you know what I'm planning for your friends, and for Treasure Island."

"Enough, *Barbecue*," I spat, tired of his Long John Silver tongue and conniving games. I felt betrayed; he had feigned an interest in me, when in fact he probably planned to slit my throat along with Dr. Livesey and the others. "I shall not be answering any more inquiries from a common corsair like you, and I warn you, if you take one step towards me I shall scream mutiny, and the entire company of this ship shall hear it. Your plan will be exposed quicker than a sail unfurling."

"I wouldn't do that, if I were you," said Long John Silver, raising one finger to indicate that caution would be prudent. "My loyal men outnumber your friends three-to-one. If you shout mutiny, you would seal their fates, and yours as well."

"You're going to kill me, anyway," I said. "I've had enough encounters with your kind already to know that much."

But as I spoke I saw something in his face turn, and suddenly there was a look of thoughtful consideration there, almost as if I could see him hatching a new plan right before my eyes. Everything I had seen of Long John Silver, from his earrings and crutch to the way he cooked to the way he manipulated everyone, revealed that his adaptability was what made him so dangerous.

At last, he spoke, his voice almost like honey. "I'm not going to kill you, Jim. And Israel here, he's not going to kill you, neither. No, in fact, I'm quite glad you heard all you did in that apple barrel. Had you not been here, I was going to come find you later and tell the same tales to your own self."

"You were?" Now it was my turn to sound incredulous.

"Yes, Jim, it's only reasonable. You're the good lad who found the map, are you not? We need you to lead us to the treasure. You're trusted by the squire and his men. You could make them drop their guard. We need you, Jim. I want you to join our side."

It was unfathomable. Join the pirates? How could I betray Dr. Livesey and Squire Trelawney after all they had given me? Then again, the gentlemen had seemed quite eager to have at my map. They were downright amused reading it, saying they'd be rich and all that. I was the one who found the map.

By rights, it was mine. Was I really sure that once the treasure was found, the gentlemen would grant me a share at all?

"I don't have time for you to flap in the breeze," Long John said. "You need to anchor somewhere. I hope it'll be with me and mine. What's it going to be?"

If you would agree to join the pirates, turn to page 163

If you would pretend to agree to join the pirates, turn to page 178

If you would refuse to join the pirates, turn to page 155

ong John wanted my help saving him from the gallows once all was said and done.

"What I can do, I'll do," I said, though I could not see how I could convince anyone not to hang this old buccaneer, the ringleader of the whole mutiny.

"It's a bargain," cried Long John. "Now, Jim, please tell me, do you have any idea why the doctor would give me the treasure map?"

My face expressed pure wonder, revealing to him that I was as ignorant to the answer as he was.

"Ah, well, he did," said Silver. "And there's something under that, no doubt—something, surely, under that, Jim— bad or good."

And he shook his great fair head like a man who looks forward to the worst.

Turn to page 30

*T*hough my knees were like marmalade, my feet were stuck fast upon the floor. I did not want anyone coming to harm under my mother's roof, and yet I did not have the courage to intervene.

The doctor never so much as moved. He spoke to the captain as before, over his shoulder and in the same tone of voice, rather high, so that all the room might hear, but perfectly calm and steady: "If you do not put that knife this instant in your pocket, I promise, upon my honor, you shall hang the next time the courts are in session."

I held my breath, fearful of how the captain might reply.

Turn to page 116

*T*hough it did not feel honorable to spit in Long John Silver's face, it did feel good to defy him. He howled in anger, wiped phlegm from the corner of his eye, and slammed his fist down on an ale barrel.

"Harry! Morgan! Get in here, you rats!" He screamed oaths at me and swung his crutch violently in the air. I couldn't help but laugh.

The other pirates entered the storeroom, pushing past Long John, and grabbed me as I kicked and scratched and bit them. I screamed for help, but who knows if anyone could hear me through the door and the loud din of the tavern.

"You've made the lawful choice, Jimmy," Silver hissed. "Now I'll show you how pirate law deals with enemies."

Morgan pried open one of the barrels of ale as Harry grabbed me about the waist and lifted me, then dumped me headfirst into the open barrel. The sour, foul-smelling brew doused me as the barrel overflowed and spilled onto the floor.

As I splashed and flailed, the pirates forced my head down and fitted the lid back on top of the barrel. I was underwater, drowning in the noxious, fermented ale. I could hear them hammering nails down into the lid, sealing me inside. It was the final sound I heard as my strength left me and ale poured into my lungs.

THE END

I determined to gather supplies back at the *Hispaniola* and cut the schooner adrift so that the pirates could not commandeer it and maroon us on Treasure Island as Flint had old Ben Gunn. Hurrying down the knoll to the jolly-boat, I shoved off and made my way along the coast.

When I came upon the ship, I sat to wait for darkness. After a time, the fog buried all heaven. As sunlight dwindled, absolute blackness settled down on Treasure Island. Once all was dark, I paddled to the lines that connected the anchor to the ship herself. One by one, I cut the strands until all was let loose, and the ship began to drift.

All this time I had heard the sound of loud voices from the cabin. One I recognized as the coxswain's, Israel Hands. The other wore a red night-cap and was hollering and picking fights.

Hearing their squabble, I climbed aboard to see what was the matter. But at one glance, I saw Israel Hands and his companion locked together in deadly wrestle, each with a hand upon the other's throat.

Suddenly the schooner gave a violent yaw, turning abruptly. Hands shouted, then his companion, and the two pirates had at last been interrupted in their quarrel and awakened to a sense of their disaster.

To and fro, up and down, north, south, east, and west, the *Hispaniola* sailed by swoops and dashes, and at each repetition ended as she had begun, with idly flapping canvas. The rough movements knocked me to the deck, and I lost sight of the pirates. I was so dizzy, I could not stand. Was none of the men steering?

When I reached the ship's wheel, I saw the red-cap on his back, as stiff as a handspike. Israel Hands was propped against the bulwarks, his chin on his chest, his hands lying open before him on the deck, his face as white as a tallow candle. I thought certainly they had killed each other in their argument. Dark blood had splashed upon the planks.

While I was looking, Israel Hands turned partly around with a low moan of pain and deadly weakness.

"Come aboard, Mr. Hands," I said ironically, remembering the brutal talk he had uttered when I was in the apple barrel.

He grunted. "Where might you have come from, Master Jim?"

"I've come aboard to take possession of this ship,

Mr. Hands; and you'll please regard me as your captain until further notice."

He looked at me sourly but said nothing. I pointed to the flags, where the Jolly Roger—skull and crossbones—was waving in the wind.

"By the by," I continued, "I can't have these colors, Mr. Hands; and by your leave, I'll strike 'em. Better nothing flies than these."

I ran to the flags, pulled down their cursed black flag, and chucked it overboard.

"God save the king!" said I, waving my cap. "And there's an end to Captain Silver!"

As I did this work, I noticed Mr. Hands struggle to rise. He was clearly injured, and when he thought I wasn't looking, I caught a glimpse of him slipping a dirk, or long knife, discolored to the hilt with blood, into his jacket.

Taking note of this, I went to the ship's wheel and righted her, then locked the sails and let the ship come to calmness.

"You're a good boy, Cap'n Hawkins, but good never did nothin' on the sea. For thirty years I've sailed the seas and seen good and bad, better and worse, fair weather and foul, provisions running out, knives going, and whatnot. Well, now I tell you, I never seen good come o' goodness yet. I'm one who strikes first, for dead men don't bite; them's my views."

I turned just in time to see him rush at me with the dirk in his hand. We both cried out. He threw himself forward and

I leaped sideways, and I think this saved my life, for Hands crashed headlong into the tiller and was stunned.

Before he could recover, I drew a pistol from my pocket, took a cool aim, and drew the trigger. The hammer fell, but there followed neither flash nor sound; the priming was useless with sea-water. I cursed myself for my neglect.

He now rushed at me, and circling the main mast, I sprang into the mizzen shrouds, rattled up hand over hand, and did not draw a breath till I was seated on the cross-trees. As I climbed, the dirk struck the mast not half a foot beneath my toes. I looked and saw Israel Hands below with his mouth open and his face upturned to mine, a perfect statue of surprise and disappointment.

With a moment to myself, I lost no time in changing the priming of my pistol. This work alerted Hands to the danger of his situation, and he quickly hauled himself heavily into the shrouds, with the dirk in his teeth, though he clearly was slow and struggling through the pain of his previous skirmish.

But I was aimed and ready to fire before he reached me. "One more step, Mr. Hands, and I'll blow your brains out! Dead men don't bite, you know."

He stopped instantly. I could see by the working of his face that he was trying to think. At last, he spoke. "Jim, I reckon we're fouled, you and me, and we'll have to sign articles of peace."

Just then something sang like an arrow through the air;

I felt a blow and then a sharp pang, and there I was pinned by the shoulder to the mast. In the horrid pain and surprise of the moment, my pistol went off. With a choked cry, the coxswain loosed his grasp upon the shrouds and plunged headfirst into the water. He rose once to the surface in a lather of foam and blood and then sank again for good.

With a shudder of pain, I broke free of the knife, which had only just nicked me, and it was mostly my coat that was pinned. Once I had freed myself, I climbed back down to the deck and laid the second anchor. Inspecting the place, I saw that I was now the only living soul aboard the *Hispaniola*; I had reclaimed it for King, Country, and Captain.

Thus I decided to return to the island. I was curious how the others were getting on, and I still wanted to know the secrets Ben Gunn had to share. I would take the jolly-boat back to shore and begin my search in earnest from there.

Turn to page 62

As Squire Trelawney had suggested, we made haste for the *Hispaniola*, which lay some way out from the other ships. They had cables strewn like a crisscross of spiderwebs, thick, heavy threads that swung above us and sometimes grated underneath our keel. As we stepped aboard the vessel, we were met and saluted by Mr. Arrow, a brown old sailor with earrings in his ears and a squint. He and the squire were very thick and friendly, but I soon observed that things were not the same between Mr. Trelawney and the captain of the *Hispaniola*.

The captain was a sharp-looking man who seemed very angry with everything on the ship, and did not hesitate to tell us why. He followed us down into the cabin and shut the door behind him.

"Well, Captain Smollett," the squire said with a smile. "What have you to say? Are we all shipshape and seaworthy?"

"It's best I speak plain," the captain rejoined, "even at the risk of offense. I don't like this cruise; I don't like the men; and I don't like my officer. That about covers everything."

"Oh does it?" asked the squire in an irritated fashion. "Are you sure you don't dislike the ship as well? What about your employer?"

"I can't speak to the ship, as I have not seen her out of port," said the captain. "She seems a clever craft. And as for you—"

Livesey cut in, perhaps sparing us all more theatrics. "Why do you dislike the cruise, Captain?"

"The squire engages me with sealed orders, sir, to sail this ship anywhere I am bidden. So far so good. But then I learn we are after treasure, and learn it from my own hands. I don't like treasure voyages, and I don't like secret treasure voyages, and I don't like secret treasure voyages that are only secret to me!"

"I swear, I told no one," said the squire, his cheeks flushed.

"We will find out who has been spreading this news around, and we apologize to you, Captain Smollett." Dr. Livesey cleared his throat. "Now, you say you don't like the crew? And Mr. Arrow?"

"I don't like the men," Captain Smollett said. "I prefer to have the choosing of my own hands. And Arrow is a good seaman, but he's too free with the crew to be a good officer. A good first mate should keep to himself."

The captain nodded to each of us, even me. "Now, you

have heard me patiently, and I am grateful for that. But there is one other matter about the map."

"How do you know about the map?" asked the squire, flabbergasted.

"Everyone knows, sir," said the captain. "That is my point. Every man aboard this ship could recite the latitude and longitude to you from memory. I think you should make a garrison of the stern part of this ship, stockpile our munitions there, man it only with the squire's own people, and provide them all with arms and powder while aboard. And the map shall be kept secret even from me and Mr. Arrow. Otherwise, I would ask that you let me resign."

"You fear a mutiny," said the doctor. It wasn't a question.

"I would not join this voyage if that were wholly true, but I have concerns."

"Captain Smollett," the doctor said, "thank you for your candor. We will take your advice with the utmost seriousness and do as you desire."

"Yes," agreed the squire. "But I think the worse of you."

"That's as you please, sir," said the captain. "You'll find I do my duty."

And with that he took his leave.

"Trelawney," said the doctor, "contrary to all my notions, I believe you have managed to get two honest men on board with you—that man and John Silver."

"Silver, if you like," cried the squire; "but as for that

intolerable humbug, I declare I think his conduct unmanly, unsailorly, and downright un-English."

"Well," said the doctor, "we shall see."

When we came on deck, the men had begun already to rearrange the ship to the captain's preferred calibration, and Mr. Arrow stood superintending. The new arrangement was quite to my liking, with much more space to stretch out. Dr. Livesey, Squire Trelawney, his men Hunter, Redruth, Joyce, and myself were to sleep in our little garrison. The captain and Mr. Arrow would sleep on deck in the companion.

Neither the squire nor Long John Silver seemed totally pleased with this arrangement, but their resentment seemed not to bother the captain one bit. A little before dawn, the boatswain sounded his pipe and the crew began to man the capstan-bars.

"Tip us a stave!" cried one voice.

"The old one," cried another.

"Aye, aye, mates," said Long John, who was standing by, with his crutch under his arm, and at once broke out in the air and words I knew so well:

"Fifteen men on the dead man's chest—"

And then the whole crew bore chorus:

"Yo-ho-ho, and a bottle of rum!" And on the third "ho!" drove the bars before them with a will.

Soon the anchor was up, and the *Hispaniola* had begun her voyage to the Isle of Treasure.

I am not going to relate the voyage in full detail. It was fairly prosperous. The ship proved to be a good ship, the crew were capable seamen, and the captain thoroughly understood his business. But before we came the length of Treasure Island, two or three things happened which require to be known.

Mr. Arrow, first of all, turned out even worse than the captain had feared. He had no command among the men, and people did what they pleased with him. But that wasn't even the worst of it. After a day or two at sea, he began to appear on deck with hazy eye, red cheeks, and stuttering tongue. Multiple times Captain Smollett ordered him below in disgrace. Sometimes Mr. Arrow fell and cut himself; sometimes he lay all day long in his little bunk at one side of the companion.

It seemed that something very suspicious was afoot with Mr. Arrow, but short of scolding him and gossiping about him, no one aboard the *Hispaniola* seemed interested in getting to the bottom of the mate's erratic behavior. I wondered if I should follow his movements and see what I could learn.

If you would spy on Mr. Arrow,
turn to page 150

If you would leave Mr. Arrow be,
turn to page 185

"Come, you lot," I said. "Don't let that voice scare you. Let's keep moving up the hill and find that treasure."

"Jim is right," said Silver, struggling with his ashen lips to get the words out; "this won't do. Stand by to go about. I can't name the voice, but it's someone skylarking—someone that's flesh and blood, and you may lay to that."

It was extraordinary how their spirits had returned after this encouragement, and not long after, hearing no further sound, they shouldered the tools and set forth again. We crossed the summit, circled around the hill, and came upon a tree so immense that none of us doubted seven hundred thousand pounds in gold lay somewhere buried below its spreading shadow. From time to time Silver would turn his eyes upon me with a deadly look. I could read his face like print. All his promises were forgotten—all his kindness. He would slit any throat to get those riches and get to safety.

We hurried down into the thicket, and the foremost pirate

broke into a run. The others took off after him. "Huzza, mates, all together!" shouted Merry.

But suddenly, not ten yards further, they stopped. A low cry arose. Silver doubled his pace, digging away with the foot of his crutch like one possessed. The next moment he and I came to a dead halt.

Before us was a great excavation, not very recent, for the sides had fallen in and grass had sprouted on the bottom. In the pit were the shaft of a broken pick and the boards of several packing-cases. On one of these boards I saw, branded with a hot iron, the name *Walrus*—the name of Flint's ship.

The emptiness of the pit made it clear. The cache had been found and rifled; the seven hundred thousand pounds were gone!

The pirates stopped short, as though they had been struck, but with Silver the blow passed almost instantly. He kept his head, found his temper, and changed his plan before the others could realize their disappointment.

"Jim," he whispered, "take that, and stand by for trouble."

And he passed me a double-barreled pistol.

At the same time, he started moving around the treasure pit so that it was between us two and the other five. "We're in a narrow corner, Jim," he said, and indeed it was.

"So have you changed sides again?" I was so revolted by his constant changes that I couldn't resist sticking it to him.

But there was no time for him to reply. The buccaneers,

with oaths and cries, began to leap, one after another, into the pit and to dig with their fingers, throwing the boards aside as they did so. Morgan found a piece of gold. He held it up with a perfect spout of oaths. It was a two-guinea piece, and it went from hand to hand among them for a quarter of a minute.

"Two guineas!" roared Merry, shaking it at Silver. "That's your seven hundred thousand pounds, is it? You said you never bungled nothing, you wooden-headed lubber!"

Silver sneered and mocked the man, but the others were entirely in Merry's favor. They scrambled out of the excavation, darting furious glances behind them, then there we stood, two on one side, five on the other, the pit between us, and nobody screwed up tight enough to offer the first blow. Silver never moved; he watched them, very upright on his crutch, and looked as cool as ever I saw him.

At last Merry seemed to think a speech might help matters.

"Mates," said he, "there's two of them and five of us; one's the old cripple and the other's that cub, and I mean to have that cub's heart. Now, mates—"

He plainly meant to lead a charge, but just then—*crack! crack! crack!*—three musket-shots flashed out of the thicket. Merry tumbled headfirst into the excavation; the man with the bandage spun round like a top and fell all his length upon his side, where he lay dead but still twitching; and the other three turned and ran for it with all their might.

At the same moment, the doctor, Gray, and Ben Gunn

joined us, with smoking muskets, from among the nutmeg-trees.

"Forward!" cried the doctor. "Double quick, my lads. We must head 'em off."

And we set off at a great pace, sometimes plunging through chest-high bushes, but when we saw the survivors running right for Mizzenmast Hill, with nowhere else to go, we four sat down to breathe, while Long John, mopping his face, came slowly up with us on his crutch.

"Thank ye kindly, doctor," said he. "You came in the nick, I guess, for me and Hawkins. And so it's you, Ben Gunn!" he added. "Well, you're a nice one, to be sure."

"I'm Ben Gunn, I am," replied the maroon, wriggling like an eel in his embarrassment. "And how do, Mr. Silver?"

The doctor sent back Gray for one of the pick-axes deserted by the mutineers, and we proceeded leisurely downhill to where the *Hispaniola* was anchored, relating in a few words what had taken place. Ben Gunn was the hero from beginning to end.

In his long, lonely wanderings about the island, Ben had found the skeleton, which led him to the treasure. He had dug it up and had carried it on his back, in many weary journeys, from the foot of the tall pine to a cave he had on the two-pointed hill at the northeast angle of the island. There it had lain in safety for quite some time before the arrival of the *Hispaniola*.

In my absence, the doctor had met Ben Gunn, as I had, and wormed the secret from him. Thus, it was easy for the doctor to give Silver the chart (useless) and the stores, for Ben had stored salted goat meat aplenty in his cave. Once the pirates were on the trail of the empty treasure trove, it was a simple matter of laying an ambush.

"So it's a good thing I had Hawkins with me," said Silver. "You would have let old John be cut to bits, and never given it a thought, Doctor."

"Not a thought," replied Dr. Livesey cheerily.

As we reached the shore, the squire met us. To me he was cordial and kind, saying nothing of my escapade either in the way of blame or praise. At Silver's polite salute he somewhat flushed.

"John Silver," he said, "you're a prodigious villain and impostor—a monstrous impostor, sir. The dead men, sir, hang about your neck like millstones."

The squire led us to Ben Gunn's cave. We entered. It was a large, airy place, with a little spring and a pool of clear water, overhung with ferns. The floor was sand. Before a big fire lay Captain Smollett; and in a far corner, only duskily flickered over by the blaze, I beheld great heaps of coin and quadrilaterals built of bars of gold. That was Flint's treasure we had come so far to seek and that had cost already the lives of twenty-one men from the *Hispaniola*. How many it had cost in the amassing, what blood and sorrow, what good ships scuttled in the deep, what brave men walking the plank blindfolded, what shot of cannon, what shame and lies and cruelty, perhaps no man alive could tell. Yet there were still three upon that island—Silver and old Morgan and Ben Gunn—who had each taken his share in these crimes, as each had hoped in vain to share in the reward.

"Come in, Jim," said the captain. "And John Silver! What brings you here?"

"Come back to my duty, sir," returned Silver.

And there we celebrated our fortune, feasting and relaxing for the first time in far too long. The next morning, we fell early to work, transporting the great mass of gold to the beach and subsequently the ship. We kept up a sentry to ensure the remaining pirates didn't encroach upon us.

Day after day this work went on steadily; by every evening a fortune had been stowed aboard, but there was another fortune waiting for the morrow; and all this time we heard nothing of the three surviving mutineers. When it was finally time to go, we left what stores we could for the three men, and abandoned them to their fate on the now treasure-less island.

That was, at least, the end of that; and before noon, to my inexpressible joy, the highest rock of the island had sunk into the blue round of sea.

Turn to page 20

I had to know for sure what the source of this strange voice was. It couldn't possibly be a true specter or ghost, could it?

While the pirates mewled and shook with fear, I slipped the line that Long John Silver had used to tether me to him and set off across the gravelly hillside in the direction the voice had come from. I made quick work of that hillside, galloping across it like one of the goats Ben Gunn had subsisted on for three years, eager to learn the truth about the voice, and eager moreover to rid myself of my piratical company.

I heard the voice again as I approached a wide dark cave in the hillside. It sang loudly and raucously.

> *"Fifteen men on a dead man's chest—*
> *Yo-ho-ho and a bottle of rum."*

As I listened at the cave's mouth, I heard other voices join in with the haunting chorus. I couldn't wait any longer, in spite of my fears; I ventured into the cave.

To my surprise, the cave was lit with torches that flickered from sconces in the walls. I followed the sounds of singing until I reached an empty chamber, a dead end, and yet the howls of the song still echoed around me.

All at once, seven beings appeared, floating in the air and translucent as a rum bottle. They had no legs, rather below their belts their bodies tapered into wispy points.

"Apparitions!" I exclaimed, cowering at the sight of the ghosts.

"I am the ghost of Captain Flint . . . ," wailed one of the specters. "Who dares trespass on my island?"

Shivering in my literal timbers, I confessed, "It is I, Jim Hawkins, cabin-boy aboard the good ship *Hispaniola*."

"These are my poor dead men," said the ghost. "Not fifteen, but six is enough. I killed them here on this island, and as punishment for my treachery, they have brought my spirit here to suffer eternally. Now we cannot rest, only torment the living and seek to bring them closer to our current state of afterlife."

"Well, I humbly request that you do not bring me to such a state!" I said. "I have come to this island with many pirates, Captain Flint, some of your old crew, even. I can lead you to them. Maybe we can scare them off together."

"Scare them, yes, hmm . . . that is what ghosts do, isn't it? Scare mortal men?" The ghost of Captain Flint stroked his scraggly beard. "All right, boy, lead us to these dogs."

I showed the ghosts the way, back through the cave, step, step, step, while they howled hauntingly all around me. The ghosts became nearly invisible in the daylight as we emerged from the cave, but their howls made it easy enough to track where they floated. I showed them across the hillside to where the pirates were spread out, apparently searching for their escaped captive.

"Well, if it isn't Long John Silver!" screeched the ghost of Captain Flint. "How about I take the other leg?"

"Old Morgan!" wailed another ghost. "Let me hurry you along to the afterlife."

The pirates screamed like the devil himself had fallen into their laps (and perhaps he had). They ran as far and as fast as they could. The ghosts chased, and I followed. Unbelievably, Silver wasn't the slowest among them, even on his crutch. My heart sank as I saw the pirates approaching a steep bluff that plummeted into the sea.

"Run! Run, you lubbers!" the ghosts sang. In their delirious terror, the pirates ran directly off the edge of the bluff and plummeted hundreds of feet into the sea. We watched until moments later when their lifeless bodies bobbed to the surface, every one of them.

"They're gone, they're all gone," I said in disbelief.

"Yes, yes indeed they are," said the ghost of Captain Flint. "And we're quite glad to have had your help in this matter, Jim."

"Well, I'm very glad to have been of assistance, Captain Flint." I didn't exactly like the company of these ghosts, but it was probably unwise to let them know that.

"In fact," said the captain, "we are enjoying your company so much, we want you to join us *permanently*."

"I see, sir," said I, "but I will need to be meeting up with my friends now. They'll be expecting me." When I saw the murderous anger in the ghosts' eyes, and they moved closer, and backed me against the edge of the bluff, I added, "Of course, I could make a little time to give you all company."

"Good," hissed Captain Flint. "You can start by becoming one of us. Only ghosts are allowed to join our immortal crew."

"What? No!" I held up my hands defensively, but my foot slipped, and I plummeted down, down, down, into the dark and murky ocean.

THE END

As a guest of the inn, I could not betray the captain to this sordid stranger, however much a thorn he may have been to my family. I refused to reveal his whereabouts. "If your only purpose here is to stalk the other guests, then I suggest you be on your way, sir."

"Aye, on my way, yes, but perhaps I'll linger just a while more, in case my mate Bill happens to arrive." The stranger kept hanging about just inside the inn door, peering round the corner like a cat waiting for a mouse. At one point I stepped out into the road to fetch a pail of water, but immediately he called me back. When I did not quickly obey his fancy, a most horrible change came over his face. He ordered me in with an oath—a curse word—that made me jump.

Long, heavy moments passed, then at last the stranger said, "Ah, here's my mate Bill, with a spy-glass under his arm, bless his old 'art. Let's give Bill a little surprise, eh?"

The stranger backed along with me into the parlor and put

me behind him in the corner so that we were both hidden by the open door. I was very uneasy and alarmed, and it rather added to my fears to observe that the stranger was certainly frightened himself. He cleared the hilt of his cutlass and loosened the blade in the sheath, and all the time we were waiting there he kept swallowing as if he felt what we used to call a lump in the throat.

At last in strode the captain. He slammed the door behind him, without looking to the right or left, and marched straight across the room to where his breakfast awaited him.

"Bill," said the stranger in a voice that I thought he had tried to make bold and big.

The captain spun round on his heel and fronted us; all the brown had gone out of his face, and even his nose was blue; he had the look of a man who sees a ghost or the devil or something worse, if anything can be; and upon my word, I felt sorry to see him all in a moment turn so old and sick.

"Come, Bill, you know me; you know an old shipmate, Bill, surely," said the stranger.

The captain made a sort of gasp. "Black Dog!"

"Who else?" returned the other, getting more at ease. "Black Dog as ever was, come to see his old shipmate Billy. Ah, Bill, Bill, we have seen a sight of the times, us two, since I lost them two talons." He held up his mutilated hand.

"Now, look here," said the captain; "you've run me down; here I am; well, then, speak up; what is it?"

"I'd like to sit down, if you please, and talk square, like old shipmates."

"No, no, no, no!" the captain cried. "Enough. Speak your speech, and if it comes to swinging, swing all, say I."

Then all of a sudden, there was a tremendous explosion of oaths and other noises—the chair and table went over in a lump, a clash of steel followed, and then a cry of pain. The next instant I saw Black Dog in full flight, with the captain in hot pursuit. Both of them had cutlasses drawn, and blood streamed from Black Dog's shoulder. Just at the door, the captain aimed at the fugitive one last tremendous cut, which would certainly have split him to the chin, had it not been intercepted by our big signboard of Admiral Benbow. You may see the notch on the lower side of the frame to this day.

Once upon the road, Black Dog, in spite of his wound, disappeared over the edge of the hill in half a minute. The captain turned back inside.

"Jim," said he, "rum"; and as he spoke he stumbled and caught himself against the wall.

"Are you hurt?" cried I.

"Rum," he repeated. "I must get away from here. Rum! Rum!"

I ran to fetch it, but by the time I returned, the captain was lying full length upon the floor, unconscious. At the same instant my mother, alarmed by the cries and fighting, came running downstairs to help me. Between us we raised his head. He was breathing very loud and hard, but his eyes were closed and his face a horrible color.

"Dear, deary me," cried my mother, "what a disgrace upon the house!"

With much trouble, we managed to hoist him upstairs and laid him on his bed, where his head fell back on the pillow as if he was fainting.

Suddenly the captain opened his eyes and tried to raise himself, crying, "Where's Black Dog?"

"There's no Black Dog here," said my mother, and in a huff she turned and left the room.

Turn to page 120

*T*he indigenous population of the skull-shaped island did not seem pleased with the arrival of the *Virtue* or its crew. They manned rafts and pushed out among the rocks to our ship. The *Virtue*'s sailors defended themselves with muskets and cannons, blasting many rafts out of the water. When the rafts splintered, the sea swallowed the bodies of the attackers. But no, that wasn't right. We were the attackers. We had entered their land uninvited, and we were first to open fire. I held my breath as the remaining rafts reached the *Virtue* and their crews began to scale the hull. Soon the first warrior mounted the deck, and though Alligator Stevens was there with his machete to cut him down, more leaped aboard, and within moments we were overrun. They piled atop us and bound us with hempen rope. We were gagged and strung on poles like wild hogs caught while hunting. Then they carried us back on their rafts and up the low slope of the mountain.

Loud, deep drums thundered like the report of cannons, and manic-sounding flutes shrieked. The music of these people was violent chaos, as was all that surrounded me. I saw crewmen beaten and prodded with spears when they struggled against their ropes. I tried to stay very still, swaying slightly from my bonds as they carried me. Our captors found their way by torchlight, and in that flickering orange gleam I discovered that Captain Eaglehorn was being carried along beside me. He shouted to me, "Steady, boy, steady. Wait for the moment. We'll get out of this yet." A threatening poke from one of the spears silenced his guidance.

We reached the mountain's summit, and there a celebration was in full force. We saw dancers and chanters and several firepits among the rocks, where suckling pigs were roasting from spits identical to the one I was strung from.

One of the local people, a chief by the look of him, shouted, "Tribute! Tribute!" and pointed at each of us prisoners in turn. "Tribute!" The word was part question, part judgment, part warning of what was to come. They set their sights on the lady Fay and cut her bonds, pulling her towards a wooden obelisk that angled out over the cliff's edge.

"Not me! I don't want to!" she cried.

"Tribute?" asked the chief. Perhaps this was our last chance to volunteer to exchange fates with whatever awaited the woman. Was I to be the brave one? The others remained silent.

If you would volunteer as tribute,
turn to page 152

If you would stay silent,
turn to page 74

hat followed between the doctor and the captain was a battle of looks so tense and strained, I thought their eyes might bulge straight out of their heads and tumble into their cups, but the very next minute the captain knuckled under, put up his weapon, and resumed his seat, grumbling like a beaten dog.

"And now, sir," continued the doctor, "since I now know there's such a fellow in my district, you may count I'll have an eye upon you day and night. I'm not a doctor only; I'm a magistrate; and if I catch a breath of complaint against you, if it's only for a piece of incivility like tonight's, I'll take effectual means to have you hunted down and run out of town."

Soon after, Dr. Livesey rode away for the evening, but the captain held his peace, demonstrating his best behavior, for the remainder of the evening and for many evenings to come.

Then one frosty January morning, very early, the sun still low and only touching the hilltops and shining far to seaward, the captain rose earlier than usual and set out down the beach with his cutlass swinging under his old blue coat, his brass telescope under his arm, and his hat tilted back upon his head. I remember his breath hanging like smoke in his wake as he strode off.

I was laying the breakfast table, preparing for the captain's return, when the parlor door opened and in stepped a man I had never set my eyes on before. He was a pale, sickly creature with skin like rendered beef fat. He lacked two fingers on his left hand, and though he wore a cutlass, he did not look much like a fighter. I always had my eye open for seafaring men, with one leg or two, and this man had a smack of the sea about him.

"How can I be of service, sir?" I asked.

"Rum," came the curt reply.

I started out of the room to fetch it, but he sat down upon a table and motioned for me to draw near. I paused.

"Come here, sonny," said he. "Come nearer here."

I took a step closer.

"Is this here table for my mate Bill?" he asked with a kind of leer.

I told him I did not know his mate Bill, and this was for a person who stayed in our house whom we called the captain.

"Well," said he, "my mate Bill would be called the captain, as like as not. He has a cut on one cheek and he's mighty pleasant—in drink, I mean! So let's say that your captain has a cut on one cheek, and that cheek's the right one. Now, answer me, where is my mate Bill?"

I knew not what to say. As a guest of the Admiral Benbow inn, the captain deserved my protection, did he not? And this man seemed a sordid, treacherous fellow. And yet the captain owed my mother a good deal of coin; long ago he had drunk through the handful of gold he had paid when he first arrived. Maybe I didn't owe the captain anything, so long as he owed us so much. Maybe I should show this man where the captain usually took his walks, and let me at last be rid of him.

"Well, sonny?" the man asked. "Where be this captain of yours?"

If you would lead him to the captain, turn to page 127

If you would refuse, turn to page 109

I hesitated. I was not a killer. I was a good person. I couldn't do this to Captain Eaglehorn, who had welcomed me aboard his ship when I had been lost at sea.

"A mistake, boy," the captain spat as he kicked my legs out from under me. I fell to the ground, and he rose, weak but sure. He grabbed the rock and raised it above his bleeding head. "I'm sorry."

He dropped the rock upon my skull, and it was the last thing I ever saw.

THE END

With Mother gone, the captain rose up onto his elbows and looked me straight in the eye. "Jim," he said, "you're the only one here that's worth anything, and you know I've been always good to you. You saw that seafaring man today?"

"Black Dog?" I asked.

"Aye, Black Dog," says he. "*He's* a bad un; but there's worse that sent him here. They're going to tip me the black spot. It's my old sea-chest they're after. Go get on a horse, and go to that doctor swab, and tell him to summon all hands—magistrates and such—and have them stake out the inn. They'll be coming—all old Flint's crew, man and boy, all of 'em that's left. I was first mate, I was, old Flint's first mate, and I'm the on'y one as knows the place. He gave it me at Savannah, when he lay a-dying, just like me now, you see. That's why they're after me, Jim. And the seafaring man with the one leg! That's why they want to give me the black spot."

"But what is the black spot, Captain?" I asked.

"That's a summons, mate. A summons. Keep your weather-eye open for 'em, Jim, and I'll share with you equals, upon my honor."

He fell asleep soon after. And so things passed for days until one foggy, bitter afternoon, I saw someone drawing slowly near along the road. He was plainly blind, for he tapped before him with a stick and wore a green shade over his eyes and nose; and he was hunched, as if with age or weakness, and wore a huge old tattered sea-cloak with a hood.

He stopped a little from the inn and, raising his voice in an odd sing-song, addressed the air in front of him, "Will any kind friend inform a poor blind man, who has lost the precious sight of his eyes, where or in what part of this country he may now be?"

"You are at the Admiral Benbow, Black Hill Cove, my good man," said I.

"I hear a voice," said he, "a young voice. Will you give me your hand, my kind young friend, and lead me in?"

I held out my hand, and he gripped it like a vise. I was so startled, I struggled to withdraw, but the blind man pulled me close. "Now, boy," he said, "take me in to the captain."

"Sir," said I, "upon my word I dare not."

"Take me to him or I'll break your arm!" he sneered, wrenching it so hard that I cried out.

"Sir," said I, "it's for your own good. The captain sits with drawn cutlass. Another gentleman—"

"Come, now, march," interrupted he; and I had never heard a voice so cruel, and cold, and ugly as that blind man's. I obeyed at once, walking straight in toward the parlor, where our sick old buccaneer was sitting. The expression of his face was not so much of terror as of mortal sickness.

"Now, Bill, sit where you are," said the blind man. "If I can't see, I can hear a finger stirring. Business is business. Hold out your left hand. Boy, take his left hand by the wrist and bring it near to my right."

We both obeyed him to the letter, and he passed something from his hand into the palm of the captain's, which closed upon it instantly.

"And now that's done," said the blind man. With incredible accuracy and nimbleness, he skipped out of the parlor and into the road. I could hear his stick go tap-tap-tapping into the distance.

I looked down at the captain's palm, where there was a little round of paper, blackened on the one side. I could not doubt that this was the *black spot*. Written below in good, clear hand was this short message: "You have till ten tonight."

"Ten o'clock!" the captain cried. "Six hours. We'll have them yet." And he sprang to his feet.

Even as he did so, he reeled, put a hand to his throat, stood swaying for a moment, and then, with a peculiar sound, fell from his whole height face foremost to the floor.

I ran to him at once, calling to my mother. But haste was all in vain. The captain had been struck dead by thundering apoplexy.

My mother rushed into the room, and in a spill of urgency, I told her all that had transpired. In just a few hours, a gang of pirates would be upon us, set to steal the sea-chest, which was still upstairs, kill the captain—who was already dead— and us as well, who were still very much alive. We resolved to go forth together and seek help in the neighboring hamlet. Bare-headed as we were, we ran out at once in the gathering evening and the frosty fog.

The hamlet lay not many hundred yards away, though out of view, on the other side of the next cove. It was candle-light when we arrived, and I was cheered to see the yellow shine in doors and windows; but that cheer was the best help I was to get in that quarter, for no soul would consent to return with us to the Admiral Benbow. The more we told of our troubles, the more they clung to the shelter of their houses. The name of Captain Flint was well enough known to some in town and carried a great weight of terror.

Whenever one would refuse us, my mother made them a speech. "If none of the rest of you dare, Jim and I dare. Back we will go, the way we came, and small thanks to you big, hulking, chicken-hearted men. We'll have that chest open, if we die for it."

But was this truly our plan? To run headlong into danger and death, a host of cutthroats, and that cruel terror who had given the captain the black spot? What if they invaded while we were still inside the inn? Were the contents of the sea-chest truly worth our lives?

If you would return to the inn,
turn to page 171

If you would stay in the hamlet,
turn to page 78

r. Livesey was right; I was small and young and would be of no use to these men in the heat of battle. If I left the log-house to gather supplies, I could return with fresh food and perhaps information.

Picking up a cutlass for defense, I departed opposite the direction in which Silver had left and made my way down the knoll, into the forest. It was cooler and darker here, and I had to carefully navigate through the trees. Their bark was rough and scraped my arms when I brushed against it.

I heard from the brush, the unmistakable snorting and grunting of a pig. I couldn't help but allow a smile across my face. I could almost taste the smoky flavor of roast pork and imagined I would be hailed as a conquering hero when I returned to my friends with a side of bacon.

When I parted the brush, I thought my eyes deceived me. The pig was there, sitting on its haunches, snorting melodically. It seemed to be in deep conversation with several other animals, including a frog, a rat, and a weird, blue bird-like creature. Strangest of all was that the frog wore a tiny sea-captain's hat upon its head. Were these some of Ben Gunn's companions? I made a note to ask him when next I saw him.

Suddenly losing my appetite for bacon, and wondering how my own friends were faring, I turned around and hurried back to the stockade. I returned to my post. I would not abandon them in their time of need. I entered the log-house just as the captain was giving out commands.

Turn to page 141

I decided I should show this man with the mangled hand where the captain took his walks, as he was likely as not to meet the captain when he returned in any event, and if I refused, he was likely as not to split me from belt to brow with that cutlass he wore. Wrapping my coat about me, I guided this man beyond the large rock where the captain had gone walking. I was happy to lead him away from the premises of the inn, far from my mother and my home. If the worst was to happen, and given my fortune, I had every notion to assume it was, the captain and I would be taking a mid-morning nap at the bottom of the deep blue sea.

As I said, the morning was pinching and frosty. The cove was all gray with hoar-frost, and the rippling water of the sea lapped softly on the stones. We found the captain in his usual spot, perched on the cliffs overlooking the cove, the morning winds buffeting him forward and back like a black stocking on a clothesline, as if he cared not that the toe of one boot hung over the abyss.

"Ahoy, Bill!" the stranger called over the roaring wind, a greeting that sounded not at all friendly.

The captain spun with a start; he had the look of a man who sees a specter in sunlight. "Black Dog!"

"Aye, the same. I've missed you, Bill. Alas, it's my blade that truly wants a reunion. I hate to deprive her, but I will if you tell me where it is."

"Where what is?" the captain asked as his hand slowly drifted towards the hilt of his own sword.

"The map," Black Dog hissed, pointing the tip of his cutlass at the captain's heart.

"What's this?" The captain feigned ignorance. "You must be confused, matey."

"Wrong answer," Black Dog said as he charged, running the captain through the belly before he could unhook his own weapon.

The sound that emerged from the captain's mouth was something between a gargle and a scream, a wail of surprise and dread that will long linger in my ears. He fell onto his back, dark blood erupting from his core in gentle waves, like the water against the stones.

Black Dog sighed sadly and lowered his cutlass. "Ah, Billy, you shouldn't have kept secrets from your dear old friend, but never you worry. I'm sure I'll get the answer I seek in your bunk back at the inn. I just wanted you to know, before I relieve your shoulders of your fat head, that I'm going to take the thing you died to keep from me, and I'm going to enjoy the spoils of your suffering."

A shot rang out, high and loud, echoing across the cove like the rolling beat of a drum. I shook with a start, having failed to see the captain draw the pistol from his coat. Smoke puffed from the mouths of both the captain and his weapon; his hand and its handle both sopped with the captain's blood. Black Dog stumbled, disoriented, reaching awkwardly for the hole of torn wool that had suddenly appeared in the shoulder of his coat. In his confusion, Black Dog stumbled, too close to the cliff's edge, and slipped, vanishing over the precipice.

I rushed to the edge to see where he had fallen, but when I looked down, I suddenly became frightfully dizzy and could not see Black Dog anywhere among the rocks. The captain groaned behind me, and so I turned to face him.

"Captain, I'm sorry, I'm so sorry." I rushed to his side, holding my hand over his belly to staunch his bleeding, but seeing his pallor, I knew his final voyage was not far off.

"It's all right," the captain gasped. "It's what an old drunk killer like me deserves. If you'd refused him, he'd have slit your throat."

With the last of his strength, the captain reached under his shirt and drew out a key dangling from a piece of tarry string. He pulled hard, snapping it free, and deposited it in my hand. "It's yours now," he said. "This gift and this curse. All of Captain Flint's riches . . ."

I looked down at the small key, half submerged in a palm's worth of the captain's blood. "Riches?" I asked, looking up, meeting the captain's lifeless gaze, his eyes gray as the sky. I closed my hand around the key and hurried back to the inn. My mother nearly fainted when she saw me return, hands caked with chilled blood. I washed up quickly before returning to the cliffs. We wanted to give the captain a decent burial, but the ground was too cold for either of us to dig a proper grave. We wrapped his body in blankets and carried him back to the inn, putting him in the cellar until we could summon aid from town.

Without hesitation, I climbed the stairs to the captain's room and, using the key, unlocked the sea-chest at the foot of the bed. Inside was an odd assortment of coins and keepsakes, along with a bundle of papers sewn up in oilcloth. Believing this to be what the captain had intended for me to find, I gathered it up and, at my mother's urging, set out for Dr. Livesey's home, to see what he could make of the dead captain's secrets.

Turn to page 15

I did not hesitate to leave the snake as far behind as I could, lacking any interest in continuing to engage with such a deadly enemy. I had heard tales of its famous rattle. If I got too close, death would greet me with the creature's fangs.

I had drawn near the foot of the little hill with the two peaks. Here the live-oaks grew more widely apart and seemed more like forest trees. The air, too, smelled fresher than down beside the marsh.

And here a fresh alarm brought me to a standstill with a thumping heart. From the side of the hill, which was here steep and stony, a spout of gravel was dislodged and fell rattling and bounding through the trees. My eyes turned instinctively in that direction, and I saw a figure leap with great rapidity behind the trunk of a pine. Was it a bear? A man? A monkey? I could not tell. Suddenly Silver himself appeared less terrible in contrast with this creature of the woods.

I began to retrace my steps, but instantly the figure

reappeared and began to head me off. From trunk to trunk the creature flitted like a deer, running manlike on two legs, but stooping almost double. As he ran to me, fear filled my heart, but to my wonder and confusion he threw himself on his knees and held out his clasped hands in supplication.

"Who are you?" I asked.

"Ben Gunn," he answered, and his voice sounded hoarse and awkward, like a rusty lock. "I'm poor Ben Gunn, I am; and I haven't spoke with a living soul these three years."

He was a man with pleasing features, though his skin, wherever it was exposed, was burnt by the sun. He was clothed with tatters of old ship's canvas and old sea-cloth, and this extraordinary patchwork was all held together by a system of the most various and incongruous fastenings: brass buttons, bits of stick, and loops of tarry gaskin. About his waist he wore an old brass-buckled leather belt, which was the one thing solid in his whole outfit.

"Three years!" I cried. "Were you shipwrecked?"

"Nay, mate," said he; "marooned."

I had heard the word, and I knew it stood for a horrible kind of punishment common enough among buccaneers, in which the offender is put ashore on some desolate and distant island with a little powder and shot and left behind.

"Marooned three years ago," he continued, "and lived on goats since then, and berries, and oysters. But, mate, my heart is sore for real food. You mightn't happen to have a piece of cheese about you, now? No? Well, many's the long night I've dreamed of cheese."

"If ever I can get aboard again," said I, "you shall have cheese by the stone."

He squeezed my hands and looked at my boots, showing a childish pleasure in the presence of a fellow creature. "What do you call yourself, mate?"

"Jim," I told him.

"Well, Jim, I now believe it were Providence that put me here, for I'll let you in on a secret. I'm rich!"

I now felt sure that the poor fellow had gone crazy in his solitude.

"Now, Jim, you tell me true: Is that Flint's ship you sailed in on?" he asked.

At this I believed that I had found an ally, and I answered him at once.

"It's not Flint's ship, and Flint's dead, but some of Flint's old hands are aboard."

"Not a man—with one—leg?" he gasped.

"Long John Silver?" I asked.

"Ah, Silver!" said he. "That was his name."

"He's the cook, and the ringleader, too."

"If you was sent by Long John, I'm as good as pork."

I told him the whole story of our voyage and predicament. He heard me with the keenest interest, and when I had finished, he patted me on the head.

"You're a good lad, Jim, and you're all in a clove hitch, ain't you? Well, you just put your trust in Ben Gunn—Ben Gunn's the man to do it. Would you think it likely, now, that your squire would prove a liberal-minded one in case of help?"

"Oh, Squire Trelawney is the most liberal of men," I said. "He will give you a share of the treasure, and passage home, and clothes suitable to your station, of course."

"And I could give your squire a piece or two of knowledge in exchange. For I was on Flint's ship when he buried the treasure here, and had three years stranded to explore, and I know a thing or two, wouldn't you wager?" And with that he winked and pinched me hard.

Just then, although the sun had still an hour or two to run, all the echoes of the island awoke and bellowed to the thunder of a cannon.

"They have begun to fight!" I cried. "Follow me."

I began to run towards the anchorage, my terrors all forgotten, while close at my side the marooned man in his goatskins trotted easily and lightly.

The cannon-shot was followed after a considerable interval by a volley of small arms.

Another pause, and then, not a quarter of a mile in front of me, I beheld the Union Jack flutter in the air above a wood.

As soon as Ben Gunn saw the colors he came to a halt, stopped me by the arm, and sat down.

"Now," said he, "there's your friends, sure enough."

"Far more likely it's the mutineers," I answered.

"Phooey!" he cried. "Silver would fly the Jolly Roger, make no doubt of that. No, that's your friends. There's been blows, and your friends are ashore in the old stockade that Flint made years and years ago. I won't go up there, but you should, and make sure that it really is your friends. We can meet again later when you've confirmed it's safe."

There was a loud boom, and a cannonball came tearing through the trees and pitched in the sand not a hundred yards from where we were talking. The next moment each of us had taken to his heels in a different direction.

My direction led me up the hill. Perhaps it was not wise to run towards the cannon-fire, but I believed old Ben Gunn, that the colors of my home country flying over the knoll indicated that it was indeed my friends beneath it. I hurried there and, upon reaching the sturdy log-house inside the stockade at the top of the hill, was warmly welcomed by the faithful party.

I told my tale, and they were glad for my safety, for the same could not be said for poor Redruth, who had fallen to a pirate's musket. As we talked, night fell hard, and we buried our lost companion in the sand.

Then we sat and talked together of what we were to do.

Turn to page 53

The men had a jolly laugh at poor Mr. Arrow's expense, but Captain Smollett was not laughing. It was necessary, of course, to advance one of the men. The boatswain, Job Anderson, was the likeliest man aboard, and though he kept his old title, he served in a way as mate. Mr. Trelawney had followed the sea, and his knowledge made him very useful, for he often took a watch himself in easy weather. And the coxswain, Israel Hands, was a careful, wily, experienced old seaman who could be trusted at a pinch with almost anything.

He was a great confidant of Long John Silver, and so the mention of his name leads me on to speak of our ship's cook, Barbecue, as the men called him.

Aboard ship he carried his crutch by a lanyard round his neck, to have both hands as free as possible. It was something to see him wedge the foot of the crutch against the bulkhead and, propped against it, yielding to every movement of the ship, get on with his cooking like someone safe ashore. Still more strange was it to see him in the heaviest of weather cross the deck. He had two lines rigged up to help him across the widest spaces—Long John's earrings, they were called; and he would hand himself from one place to another, now using the crutch, now trailing it alongside by the lanyard, as quickly as another man could walk. Yet some of the men who had sailed with him before expressed their pity to see him so reduced.

"He's no common man, Barbecue," said the coxswain to me. "He had good schooling in his young days and can speak like a book when so minded; and brave—a lion's nothing alongside of Long John! I seen him grapple four and knock their heads together—him unarmed."

All the crew respected him. He had a way of talking that would make anyone obedient and perform any service. He was kind to me and always seemed glad to see me in the galley, which he kept meticulously clean, even the cage with his parrot in one corner.

The parrot was named Captain Flint. Silver had named her after the famous buccaneer.

And the parrot would say, with great rapidity, "Pieces of eight! Pieces of eight! Pieces of eight!" till you wondered that it was not out of breath or till John threw his handkerchief over the cage.

In the meantime, while the squire's opinion of the captain had not improved, the captain's opinion of our ship had. In heavy weather, every man on board seemed well content. The squire saw to it that they were the most spoiled crew who had ever set sail, with frequent treats like grog and pudding and barrels of apples for anyone who had a fancy.

The captain once told Dr. Livesey that he never knew good to come from apple barrels. They spoiled the crew, and spoiled crewmen become devils. Dr. Livesey tried to explain that the nutritional value of apples was quite high. Alas, Captain Smollett would not be decoupled from his superstition.

But good did come of the apple barrel, as you shall hear, for if it had not been for that, we should have had no note of warning and might all have perished by the hand of treachery.

This was how it came about.

We had been at sea for some time, and after a long voyage we had reached what was expected to be our final day. Everyone was in the bravest spirits because we were now so near an end of the first part of our adventure.

Now, just after sundown, when all my work was over and I was on my way to my berth, it occurred to me that I should like an apple. I ran on deck. The watch was all forward looking out for the island. The man at the helm was watching the luff of the sail and whistling away gently to himself, and that was the only sound excepting the swish of the sea against the bows and around the sides of the ship.

In I got bodily into the apple barrel and found there was scarce an apple left; but sitting down there in the dark, what with the sound of the waters and the rocking movement of the ship, I had either fallen asleep or was on the point of doing so when a heavy man sat down with a crash close by. The barrel shook as he leaned his shoulders against it, and I was just about to jump up when the man began to speak. It was Silver's voice, and before I had heard a dozen words, I would not have shown myself for all the world, but lay there, trembling and listening, in the extreme of fear and curiosity, for from these dozen words I understood that the lives of all the honest men aboard depended upon me alone.

"Oh, not I," said Silver. "Flint was cap'n; I was quartermaster, along of my timber leg. The same broadside I lost my leg, old Pew lost his deadlights. It was a master surgeon, him that ampytated me—out of college and all—but he was hanged like a dog, and sun-dried like the rest, at Corso Castle. That was Roberts' men, that was, and came of changing names to their ships—*Royal Fortune* and so on. Now, what a ship was christened, so let her stay named, I says. So it was with the old *Walrus*, Flint's old ship, that I've seen amuck with red blood and fit to sink with gold."

"Ah!" cried another voice, that of the youngest hand on board, and evidently full of admiration. "He was the flower of the flock, was Flint!"

"I saved up more than two thousand after Flint. That ain't bad for a man before the mast—all safe in bank. You'll get the same or better sailing under me, I swear. Because where are old Flint's men now? Why, most of 'em aboard here, and glad to get square meals—been begging before that, some of 'em. Old Pew, as had lost his sight, and might have thought shame, spent twelve hundred pound in a year, like a lord in Parliament. Where is he now? Well, he's dead now and under hatches; but for two years before that, shiver my timbers, the man was starving! He begged, and he stole, and he cut throats, and starved at that, by the powers!"

"I guess all that treasure ain't much use, after all," said the young seaman.

"It ain't much use to fools," cried Silver. "But now, you look here: You're young, you are, but you're as smart as paint. I see that when I set my eyes on you, and I'll talk to you like a man."

You may imagine how I felt when I heard this abominable old rogue address another with the very same words of flattery he had used on me. He was a treacherous blighter, after all, Long John Silver. Whatever he was up to, it was certainly no good. I had to warn Dr. Livesey and the doctor, but could I get away without being seen?

If you would stay put,
turn to page 43

If you would make a run for it,
turn to page 81

"Doctor, you will take the door. See and don't expose yourself, and fire through the porch. Hunter, take the east side. Joyce, you stand by the west. Mr. Trelawney, you are the best shot—you and Gray will take this long north side, with the five loopholes; it's there the danger is. If they can get up to it and fire in upon us through our own ports, things would begin to look dirty. Hawkins, neither you nor I are much for shooting; we'll stand by to load and bear a hand."

As soon as the sun had climbed above our girdle of trees, it fell with full force upon the clearing and drank up the vapors. Soon the sand was baking and the resin melting in the wood of the log-house. Jackets and coats were flung aside, shirts thrown open at the neck and rolled up to the elbows; and we stood there, each at his post, in a fever of heat and anxiety.

An hour passed away.

"Hang them!" said the captain. "This is as dull as the doldrums."

Suddenly Joyce whipped up his musket and fired. The report had scarcely died away ere it was repeated and repeated from without in a scattering volley, shot behind shot, like a string of geese, from every side of the enclosure. Several bullets struck the log-house, but not one entered; and as the smoke cleared away and vanished, the stockade and the woods around it looked as quiet and empty as before.

"Stay focused," Captain Smollett urged. "If the mutineers succeed in crossing the stockade, they will take possession of any unprotected loophole and shoot us down like rats in our own stronghold."

With a loud huzza, a little cloud of pirates leaped from the woods on the north side and ran straight at the stockade. At the same moment, the fire was once more opened from the woods, and a rifle ball sang through the doorway and knocked the doctor's musket to bits.

The invaders swarmed over the fence like monkeys. The squire and Gray fired again and yet again; three men fell, one forwards into the enclosure, two back on the outside. But of these, one was evidently more frightened than hurt, for he was on his feet again in a crack and instantly disappeared among the trees.

Two had bit the dust, one had fled, four had made good their footing inside our defenses, while from the shelter of the woods seven or eight men, each evidently supplied with several muskets, kept up a hot though useless fire on the log-house.

The four who had boarded made straight for our building, shouting as they ran. We fired several shots, but no one seemed to have been hit. In a moment, they were upon us.

The head of Job Anderson, the boatswain, appeared at the middle loophole. "At 'em, all hands!" he roared.

Another pirate grasped Hunter's musket and wrenched it from his hands through the loophole, then used it to strike the fellow senseless on the floor. Another ran through the doorway and fell with his cutlass on the doctor.

Our position was utterly reversed.

"Out, lads, out!" cried the captain. "Fight 'em in the open! Cutlasses!"

I snatched a cutlass from the pile and dashed out into the sunlight. The next moment, I was face to face with Anderson. He roared and raised his sword. I leaped to one side to avoid his strike, and lost my footing in the soft sand, and rolled headlong down the slope.

Gray, following close behind me, cut down the big boatswain as he swung at me. Another was shot at a loophole. The doctor disposed of a third with his blade. Of the four who had scaled the palisade, only one remained unaccounted for, but he had abandoned his cutlass and was clambering out again with the fear of death upon him.

"Fire from the house!" cried the doctor. "And you, lads, back into cover."

But there was no need to fire. Nothing remained of the

attacking party but the five who had fallen. We returned to the house and saw the price we had paid for victory. Hunter lay beside his loophole, stunned; Joyce by his, shot through the head, never to move again; in the room's center, the squire was supporting the captain, one as pale as the other.

"The captain's wounded," said Mr. Trelawney.

"Have they run?" asked Captain Smollett.

"All that could," returned the doctor; "but there's five of them will never run again."

"Five!" cried the captain. "That leaves us five to fourteen—better odds than we had at starting."

Turn to page 157

aptain Smollett, the squire, and Dr. Livesey were talking together on the quarter-deck. I was anxious to tell them my story, but I dared not interrupt them openly. The doctor stepped away, and as soon as I was near enough to speak and not be overheard, I broke out immediately, "Doctor, get the captain and squire down to the cabin, and then make some excuse to send for me. I have terrible news."

The doctor's face changed a little, but the next moment he was master of himself again. "Thank you, Jim," he said quite loudly, "that was all I wanted to know," as if he had asked me a question.

And with that he turned on his heel and rejoined the other two. They spoke together for a little, then without a start or raise of voice, it was clear Dr. Livesey had communicated my request. The captain gave an order to Job Anderson, and then they went below.

Soon after, I was summoned. I found the three men seated

round the table in the cabin. The doctor's wig was on his lap, a clear sign that he was agitated. The stern window was open, for it was a warm night, and you could see the moon shining behind on the ship's wake.

"Now, Hawkins," said the squire, "you have something to say. Speak up."

I did as I was bid, and told the whole details of Silver's conversation. Nobody interrupted before I was done, nor did they make so much as a movement, but they kept their eyes upon my face from first to last.

"Jim," said Dr. Livesey, "take a seat."

Turn to page 181

I broke free of the one-legged man's grasp and ran out into the street. The docks were thick with people, moving about with heavy ropes and shipping crates, barrels of fish balanced on their shoulders, and the like. An opening between two sailors revealed Black Dog ducking around a corner into an alley, the shoulder of his coat stained with blood. Had he opened the wound he had received from the captain when he ran from me?

Whether foolish or brave, I approached the alley. At the far end by a wall of bricks I saw Black Dog with the one called Harry, who Long John Silver had sent to capture the brigand, but the two were sharing a pipe and a merry laugh.

"You ran out of the Spy-glass so swiftly, you looked like a landlubber rushing to relieve himself over the side of a schooner!"

"It's not funny," Black Dog snarled. "That bloody kid—I opened my stitches getting out of there."

"Not to worry. I wager old Silver is tellin' him tales, but you're not likely to have a place aboard the *Hispaniola* now."

"Black Dog!" I cried out, balling my hands into fists. "You'll hang for this, I swear it!"

But I could swear no more, for as I stood there, a large, meaty hand clamped over my mouth, and I was pulled to the ground. The one-legged man knelt on my chest, and I couldn't breathe.

"Bring him back to the Spy-glass," he ordered the other two men. "And do it quietly."

With a knife against my spine, the pirates returned me to Long John Silver's tavern, where I was taken into a back room filled with ale barrels. Hobbling on his crutch, the one-legged man moved with surprising agility. He entered behind the pirates and leaned against a barrel.

"Leave us," he growled, and the others departed. I was alone with Long John Silver now.

"I wish you hadn't done that, Jimmy," he said. "I've been working on this plan for quite a long time, paying half the fools in Bristol to keep an eye out for a landlubber lookin' to outfit a ship with haste. And there you go, spottin' old Black Dog and blowin' my cover. I'm not going to lose this chance to some wet-eared babe like you."

"On with it, then," I said, summoning what courage I could. "Slit my throat, run me through. That's what you pirates are known for, isn't it? Ending the lives of good and honest people?"

A small smile crossed his lips. He seemed unmoved by my challenge, though he tapped his crutch on the floorboards, perhaps fabricating a new plan. "You want to know what pirates are good for? I can show you, Jim. Half the squire's crew is loyal to me. We're going to take that treasure for ourselves. We could cut you in, if you're willing to keep quiet and do as I tell you."

"You want me to join you? To become a pirate?" The words did not even sound real as they came from my mouth, but Silver nodded and smiled tightly.

"It's the honest path, Jim," he said. "Many of my boys, they sailed with Captain Flint, fought and bled to earn some of that treasure for themselves. Then that crook Billy Bones made off with the map. You and your well-to-do friend, the squire, you stole that map. It's ours, by rights. We just want what we deserve.

"So what will it be, Jimmy? Can I have faith in your silence? Will you join my pirate crew?"

If you would spit in his face,
turn to page 87

If you would join the pirates,
turn to page 36

With a lazy, disrespected first mate aboard the *Hispaniola*, the whole of our voyage to Treasure Island could be in jeopardy. I did not want Mr. Arrow to be our downfall, so I set about learning the source of his erratic behavior.

One day while the ship was underway, and much of the crew was on the deck hard at work, I noticed that Mr. Arrow had retired to his little bunk to the side of the companion. I peered in, keeping quiet so that he would not spot me. He had unbuttoned his coat and was in the process of kicking off his boots. Slumping back in the bunk, he stretched out, groaning loudly and whispering oaths to himself. He fished about under the bunk and produced a bottle of amber liquid, then started tipping it into his mouth with great relief and anticipation, then tasting and swallowing with much disgust and suffering. I had seen such behavior among our patrons at the Admiral Benbow inn. Drunkenness was a sorrowful and unproductive habit, and it seemed our Mr. Arrow had fallen prey to the same vice as Billy Bones.

But where was he getting all this drink? At his rate of consumption, he would have long expended his share. Where could all this rum be coming from? It was a mystery that I hoped to solve, but as I was watching and thinking, I heard footsteps behind me of someone headed through the companion. I hurried along so as not to arouse suspicion, and did not continue my investigation after that. I regret this now, of course, because of the tragic thing that happened next.

Turn to page 185

I may have been young, but I fancied myself a proper gentleman, and I was not about to let a woman suffer grievous horror if I could shoulder that burden in her place.

"Hey!" I shouted over the deafening music. "Me! I volunteer! I'll do it! Tribute! Tribute!"

The music stopped. All around us, the locals turned and looked at me, this volunteer who was either tremendously brave or deeply stupid. Even I could not be sure which I was. They cut my bonds and pulled me bodily to the obelisk, using rope to lash me to the large spike. I was reminded of cunning Odysseus lashed to the mast of his ship, but there would be no siren songs for me to hear in this case.

Instead, the drums began to thunder once more, and I stared out into the abyss. It was hard to see in the dark, but the fires on the cliff offered a faint glimpse of a vast sea of treetops. I could see now that the jagged cliffs of the island concealed a verdant paradise at its center, but whether

I'd live to see its majesty in the light of day remained to be seen.

Boom! Boom! This was no drum but another thunderous sound that echoed through the night. What could it be? I knew not, but it was getting closer, and something was rocking the trees. I held my breath as the tree trunks parted, revealing two gleaming yellow eyes.

A massive dark hand reached out and grabbed me about the waist. I didn't even know how to react. Each finger on the hand was twice my size, and the entirety of it was covered in coarse black fur. With one swift pull, the hand snapped the obelisk off at its base and plucked me from it like one would remove a morsel from a skewer of grilled meat.

Then I was moving very quickly through the jungle, held tight in the grip of a massive creature. I had seen illustrations of monkeys in books, and this creature resembled one slightly, though it was of much heavier build, quite a bit more human, but heavyset, and of course, its size was tremendous. Seeing the magnitude of the creature, I was overcome, and fainted.

I did not wake until morning, when I found myself in something resembling a nest. The beast appeared soon after, carrying what looked like a sharp-toothed lizard the size of the *Hispaniola* over his shoulder. He broke its carcass and fed me. I ate. I was famished, and the raw lizard meat did not deter my hunger.

For many suns and many moons I stayed at the great

beast's side. He fed me, and together we hunted many monstrous creatures, including giant insects and the like. At some point—it's difficult to remember how long ago now—the crew of the *Virtue* attempted a rescue operation to save me from the beast. I'm not sure how they escaped the locals, but they had muskets and arrows and sharpened sticks. The beast crushed them all underfoot. There were no survivors.

I suppose I should have mourned my former companions, but the truth is that I had grown accustomed to the care I received from my captor. In time, I grew to love him, and saw him as my king.

THE END

"*Like hell* I'll join you scurvy pirates!" I stomped my foot upon the deck, fury in my voice. Though the risk was great, I was not about to abandon my principles to save my young life. I was not going to let Long John Silver corrupt me, and I was certainly not going to become a thieving cutthroat myself. He had wanted me to join his mutiny against the squire and Dr. Livesey. I would not agree under any circumstances.

"Are you quite sure?" Long John Silver exchanged a thick glance with his mate Israel Hands.

"Quite sure!" I replied.

Silver sighed and fixed the point of his crutch steady upon the deck, then he rose and looked down at me with a face of resigned disappointment. "Well, then, Jim, my boy, I'm going to have to ask you to get back in the apple barrel."

Before I could question the strange instruction, the coxswain leaped at me, grappled me about the middle, and flung me headfirst into the barrel.

"Help!" I cried. "Please, help me!"

"No worries, mate," said the boy, Dick, sounding friendly and helpful in deceptive contrast to his attempts to force my feet inside the barrel. "I'll help you. No one else need bother." It made sense. They were trying to make it sound like I wasn't in mortal danger.

My next cry was "Pirates! Mutiny!" But Israel had already slammed the lid down on the barrel. The coxswain said, "Hand me some nails if they're lying about, Barbecue. I've got me hammer right here."

In moments I was nailed shut inside the apple barrel, a prisoner, like some helpless, deciduous fruit. My desperate muffled cries were heard by none who was not a traitorous villain. I could not see out of the apple barrel, and with the lid sealed I could barely hear, but I felt the barrel being hoisted into the air, and the impatient grunts of Israel Hands.

For a split second I felt as if my whole body was being lifted into the air—not with the barrel, but opposite it—only to slam into the bottom of the barrel with such tremendous force that I feared the wood would splinter. Then I started rolling, end over end, helplessly. I realized that the barrel had been flung overboard with me inside, and now I was but jetsam in the ocean current.

Turn to page 165

The mutineers did not immediately redouble their assault, so we had time to tend to the wounded and see to our dinner. Out of the eight men who had fallen in the action, only three still breathed—one of the pirates, Hunter, and Captain Smollett. Of these, the first two were as good as dead; the mutineer died while the doctor attempted surgery to save him, and Hunter, do what we could, never recovered consciousness in this world. He had struck his head while falling, and some time in the following night, without sign or sound, he went to his Maker.

The captain's wounds were grievous but not dangerous. No organ was fatally injured. Job Anderson's musket-ball had broken his shoulder-blade, and another ball had torn his calf. He would recover, but the doctor said it was wise for him to neither move nor speak if he could help it.

On the other hand, I was in fine health and fair enough spirits, all things considered. I wondered if I might go out and explore a bit and perhaps find a way to help our little band in our mission. The *Hispaniola* had supplies, and there was a risk that the pirates might attempt to take her and sail her away from Treasure Island. I could row our jolly-boat and go and collect what additional supplies I could, and perhaps cut the schooner adrift, to keep anyone from leaving.

Another option was to search for Ben Gunn. The strange man, marooned—as he had said—on Treasure Island for three years, might have a camp where he ate his goats and passed his time. He had hinted also at knowing secrets of the island, and I wondered if one of these secrets would give us insight into the location or nature of Flint's treasure.

Both were enticing propositions. But where was I to go?

If you would return to the schooner,
turn to page 89

If you would look for Ben Gunn,
turn to page 62

ong John Silver wanted me to take a guess as to how the first mate Mr. Arrow met his demise, but I had long since made up my mind about the poor wretch's outcome.

"I believe as Captain Smollett does," said I. "Mr. Arrow was soused with drink—a disgusting habit—anyone who does it will face similar tragedy, mark my words."

The gathered sailors who listened to my tale removed their caps and bandannas somberly and hung their heads, nodding prudently.

Continuing, I said, "I can see it in my mind. Mr. Arrow must have had a secret stash of libation somewhere aboard, and after drinking his nightly fill, he stumbled onto the deck to relieve himself of extra moisture."

"Mr. Arrow didn't have a pot to piss in!" sniggered Job Anderson, the boatswain.

"On the contrary," I said. "Mr. Arrow had the great drink of the Atlantic, the biggest pot of them all."

"Second biggest pot," muttered Long John Silver.

I said, "Mr. Arrow's vision would be blurry, and his balance off-kilter. I've seen it myself, sirs, working at the Admiral Benbow inn. But on this choppy night, while Mr. Arrow was sitting with his stern over the port side, a wave crashed, the ship tipped, and Mr. Arrow tumbled overboard. Would anyone have heard his cries? Or would he have been pulled under and scraped against the keel? A tragedy, in any case, but certainly not unexpected."

A mournful silence was the only reply as the men hung their heads. Then suddenly—

"You're awfully morbid for a cabin-boy!" jeered one of the men. The others laughed uproariously.

Turn to page 136

The boy, Dick, neared the apple barrel where I was concealed. If I stayed put, Long John Silver, Israel Hands, and Dick—traitorous pirates all—would discover me when Dick opened the barrel. But if I ran, they would see me leap out of the barrel, and I would be discovered for sure. All I could do was sit and hope.

But just then a sort of brightness fell upon the barrel, and looking up, I found the moon had risen and was shining white of the luff of the fore-sail; and almost at the same time the voice of the lookout shouted, "Land ho!"

There was a great rush of feet across the deck. I could hear people tumbling up from the cabin and the forecastle. Long John Silver, Israel Hands, and the boy, Dick, hurried to join them. I slipped in an instant outside my barrel and dove behind the fore-sail, made a double towards the stern, and came out upon the open deck in time to join Dr. Livesey and Hunter, one of the squire's men. Could it really be that we had found Treasure Island at last? I approached the weather bow to find out.

Turn to page 48

ilver spoke the truth. It was right to join the pirates. The squire and doctor had taken advantage of me for too long. The treasure was mine, by rights, and Long John Silver was going to help me get it.

"All right," I said with determination. "I am with you, you criminal lot. Let me get a cutlass, and I'll join the mutiny."

"What? Jim! Say it isn't so." The doctor sounded horrified, but not more than I must have looked as I turned to see him flanked by the captain and the squire.

"We overheard the whole thing," the captain said. "And now it'll be irons for the lot of you. Even you, Jim Hawkins. How you could be corrupted by this brigand is beyond me."

I thought perhaps that their minds would change overnight. I was, after all, a mere boy. But justice had different plans and I had trusted the wrong man.

It was a fatal error, for at dawn a board was laid out

over the open ocean. Sharks circled, and one by one we mutinous pirates were prodded with swords until we stood at the end of the plank, and one by one we fell beneath the waves.

THE END

ealed inside an empty apple barrel, blind to the outside world, lost at sea, adrift, victim of the mutinous dog, Long John Silver, I would be lying if I did not say that I wished for death. My head and body had suffered grievous wounds as the waves tossed me roughly from one side of the barrel to the other, and though it embarrasses me to admit, I did make a mess of the barrel when seasickness overtook me. The barrel was watertight (thankfully, as I would have promptly drowned otherwise), but consequently there was nowhere for the mess to go. It was certainly the worst experience of my life, as hours if not days passed in the barrel. I was starving and filthy, and the stench was something atrocious. Had my body the strength, I would have broken the barrel with swift kicks and ended it all. Instead, I drifted into unconsciousness and submitted to my fate.

But then . . . light! I heard the squeak of nails being pulled and the splintering of wood. I opened my foggy eyes to the painful light of the sun. I felt hands on me as they pulled my limp, frail body from the apple barrel and deposited me on a clean, soft blanket. I could feel the firmness of the ground below—the deck of a ship—and the gentle swaying of the sea.

Blurry shapes hovered in my vision, and as my eyes regained focus, I saw that the shapes were faces—the faces of several seafaring men and boys.

"Oy, look at that!" said one of the lads. "It's a kid!" The lad spoke something like the king's English, but he had the most peculiar accent, as if all of the dignity had been taken out of the language.

"Captain!" called one of the adults. "There was a boy in that barrel we fished aboard."

"A boy?" came a stern and intelligent voice. "Such a pity. Wrap him and we'll have a proper burial."

"No, Captain!" said the first man. "The boy's alive!"

There was a great rush of activity as the men carried me into the shade and helped me to a sitting position. I was still very weak and could barely lift a hand. Someone put a ladle of water to my lips, and I drank desperately.

A tall man with broad shoulders approached me. He wore something like a captain's uniform, but the color was off, and the adornments were impossible to recognize.

"Are you all right, boy?" he asked, sounding concerned. "What's your name?"

"Jim Hawkins, sir."

"I'm Captain Eaglehorn of the good ship *Virtue*, out of Boston."

"The colonies! I was aboard the *Hispaniola*, from Bristol. There was a mutiny, sir. Pirates among the crew betrayed us, and I was tossed overboard."

"Cursed pirates! I'll put in word to the authorities when next we reach port. But for now, you must rest and have some food in you. Welcome aboard the *Virtue*, Jim Hawkins. I'm glad we saved your life."

They fed me well, with toast and preserves and even some pickled herring. They had apples, as well, but I'd had enough of apples. I had to be careful and eat slowly, for I had gone so long without a meal that my stomach felt knotted and delicate. The men watched me as I ate, as if I were some strange curiosity to be marveled at.

"It's a miracle that you survived," said the ship's cook, a big, swarthy man with a mustache and a great deal of grizzled stubble on his cheeks. His arms were thick as country hams and covered in tattoos. The men called him Stewbeef. "The boys ain't used to witnessin' miracles."

The cabin-boy offered me his hammock next to the cook, and I slept for nearly a day, until the pain in my stiff joints had begun to subside. It felt good to stretch out again, with straight legs and back.

The next morning, Captain Eaglehorn summoned me to his cabin. "It's good to see you well rested, Jim Hawkins. You look half human again." He sat behind his desk, feet up, hat resting on his boot. "We're going to need to discuss your presence on the *Virtue*. You see, this voyage was commissioned to explore an uncharted island. We believe it has native inhabitants, and several of my passengers hope to explore the place for riches."

Nervously I asked him what the coordinates of this island were. To my relief, it was not Treasure Island.

"We must make for the island with haste," said the captain. "So you must choose. Will you come with us to this mysterious island? Or would you prefer to be left at the nearest port? We will drop you off and pick up some additional supplies. It is a miracle you survived your ordeal in the apple barrel, Jim Hawkins. The men would think it bad luck to not attend to your needs here, whatever they may be."

So I had a choice. The *Virtue* was sailing into danger, and I could join them if I wished, but I would risk escaping the frying pan only to fall directly into the fire. What was I to do?

If you would go to the mysterious island, turn to page 57

If you would go to the nearest port, turn to page 23

I decided to go ashore. In a jiffy I had slipped over the side and curled up in the fore-sheets of the nearest boat, and almost at the same moment she shoved off.

No one took notice of me, only the bow oar, who said, "Is that you, Jim? Keep your head down." But Silver, from the other boat, looked sharply over and called out to know if that were me; and from that moment I began to regret what I had done.

My boat was the first to reach the beach. I caught a branch and swung myself out and plunged into the nearest thicket, while Silver and the rest were still a hundred yards behind.

"Jim, Jim!" I heard him shouting, but I paid no heed—jumping, ducking, and breaking through the trees until I could run no longer.

I was so pleased at having given the slip to Long John that I began to enjoy myself and look around with some interest at this strange land.

I crossed a marshy tract full of willows and swampy trees and came out upon the skirts of an open piece of undulating, sandy country. Though somewhat free, there was not joy in my exploration. The isle was uninhabited; my shipmates I had left behind, and nothing lived in front of me but birds and beasts of the wild. I saw unknown plants, and here and there were snakes. One raised its head from a ledge of rock and hissed at me with a noise not unlike the spinning of a top.

"Hello there, serpent," I greeted the reptile. It flicked its tongue at me, almost as if it were waving. I wondered if I could gain the alliance of such a creature. It seemed to like my company. Perhaps it would protect me from the pirates?

If you would befriend the snake,
turn to page 61

If you would leave the snake alone,
turn to page 131

Of course I said I would go with my mother, back to the inn, to retrieve the chest, and of course the townspeople all cried out at our foolhardiness, but even then not a man would go along with us.

We hurried home along the hedges, noiseless and swift. When the door of the Admiral Benbow had closed behind us, I slipped the bolt, and my mother got a candle from the bar. We advanced into the parlor. The dead captain lay as we had left him, on his back, with his eyes open and one arm stretched out.

"Draw down the blind, Jim," whispered my mother; "they might come and watch outside. And now, we have to get the key off *the body*."

I felt in his pockets, one after another. A few small coins and a pocket compass was all, and I began to despair.

"Perhaps it's round his neck," suggested my mother.

Overcoming a strong repugnance, I tore open his shirt at the neck, and there, sure enough, hanging on a bit of tarry string, which I cut with his own gully knife, we found the key. At this triumph we were filled with hope and hurried upstairs without delay to the little room where he had slept so long and where his box had stood since the day of his arrival.

It was like any other seaman's chest on the outside, the initial "B" burned on the top of it with a hot iron and the corners somewhat smashed and broken as by long, rough usage.

My mother took the key and unlocked it, throwing back the lid in a twinkling.

There was nothing to be seen except a suit of very good clothes, carefully brushed and folded. They had never been worn, my mother said. Under that, the miscellany began, shells and trinkets, but nothing of value other than a piece of silver bar. Underneath, there was an old boat-cloak, whitened with sea-salt on many a harbor-bar. My mother pulled it up impatiently, and there lay before us, the last things in the chest, a bundle tied up in oilcloth, and looking like papers, and a canvas bag that gave forth, at a touch, the jingle of gold.

"I'll show these rogues that I'm an honest woman," said my mother. "I'll have my dues, and not a farthing over. Hold the bag, Jim." And she began to count over the amount of the captain's score from the sailor's bag into the one that I was holding.

When we were half-way through, I heard in the silent frosty air a sound that brought my heart into my mouth— the tap-tapping of the blind man's stick upon the frozen road. Then it struck sharp on the inn door, and then we could hear the handle being turned and the bolt rattling as the wretched being tried to enter. For a long time there was silence, and then the tapping began again and died slowly away until it ceased to be heard.

"I'll take what I have," Mother said, jumping to her feet.

"And I'll take this to square the count," said I, picking up the oilskin packet.

The next moment we had opened the front door and were in full retreat. The fog was rapidly dispersing, and the moon shone quite clear on the road. The sound of several footsteps running came to our ears, and looking back in their direction, we could see a lantern light advancing.

We took cover down the bank on the side of the road, and our enemies began to arrive, seven or eight of them, running hard. Two of them guided the blind man between them, hand in hand.

"Down with the door!" the blind man cried.

"Aye, aye, sir!" answered two or three, and they proceeded to slam themselves through the door of the Admiral Benbow.

"In, in, in!" shouted the blind man, cursing his companions for their delay.

Some ran in, and a moment later, they ran out again.

"Pew," one cried, "they've been before us. Someone's cleaned out Billy's chest."

"Is it there?" roared Pew.

"The money's there."

"To hell with the money! Find that boy! Tear this place apart!" He struck his stick upon the road.

"Hang it, Pew, we've got the doubloons!" grumbled one.

This quarrel was the saving of us, for while it was raging, a pistol-shot, flash and bang, came from the hedge side. The buccaneers turned at once and ran. In half a minute, none remained but Pew. They had deserted him. He stumbled about, crying, "Boys! Gents! Don't leave old Pew, mates—not old Pew!"

Just then four or five riders swept down the slope at a full gallop.

Hearing this, Pew ran, but in his bewilderment, ran right under the nearest of the coming horses. The rider tried to save him, but in vain. Down went Pew with a cry that rang high into the night. He was trampled. He fell on his side, then collapsed upon his face and moved no more. Pew was dead, stone dead.

One of the lads in the village had gone to Dr. Livesey's and returned with revenue officers whom he had met along the way. We were saved!

When the men heard my tale, they insisted I hurry on at once to Dr. Livesey's and report all I had witnessed at the Admiral Benbow inn.

Turn to page 15

As I stared down at Captain Eaglehorn, fallen in our battle to the death, I realized that even if I were to spare the captain's life, our captors would not look kindly upon my act of mercy. They may kill me in disgust or disappointment. They may kill the captain for losing, committing the act that I could not. More than anything, the captain seemed resigned to his fate. As I looked into his eyes, it was almost as if he was begging me to do it. He wanted me to live.

I closed my eyes and brought the rock down with all my strength. The crowd's cheers could not drown out the horrible sound. I was in a daze. They pulled me from the pit. They threw me in a cage with the other victorious crewmen of the *Virtue*. "Good job, boy," Alligator Stevens told me in a grim voice. "You lived. That's all that matters. We'll get out of this somehow, mate."

Sleep did not aid me that night. When dawn came, I heard

a tremendous howl so vicious that it threatened to split my head in two. I covered my ears, but still it penetrated.

I looked through the bars of my cage and saw a beast of monstrous size, taller than trees, with soot-colored fur. The lady Fay was riding on its shoulder! It appeared that she had tamed the beast, for it made short work of our captors, knocking them aside with its massive hands like a spoiled child throws tin soldiers.

With our captors distracted, Alligator Stevens and I kicked open our cage and crawled out. Bart Snidley was standing there in disbelief. "Look at that monkey!" he exclaimed. "I'm going to put that thing in a play! People will pay a fortune to see it!"

Indeed, the beast devastated our captors' camp at the woman's command, and then it willingly boarded the *Virtue* and joined us on our journey back to the colonies. Bart Snidley advertised his show as *The Monster of the Island of the Skull*; Fay and the beast co-starred; and as Bart Snidley narrated, he claimed it was beauty that made the beast kill.

THE END

ot in this life, the next, or ten thousand years would I betray my friends and join this wretched pirate, but I was smart enough to know what a cutthroat like Long John Silver would do to a moral lad like me—why, he'd cut my throat! Was it death or piracy, then?

No, there was a third option. Perhaps it was not the most moral choice, but it was in service of the greater good. If I did not pretend to join the buccaneers and in so doing deceive the pirate Silver, my friends would fall victim to a mutiny. I had to pretend to join them, and so that's just what I did.

"Yar, I be joinin' ye scurvy dogs. Any who cross me or deny my share'll end up at the vengeful end of my cutlass."

"That's my boy!" Silver applauded, quite amused by my display, though Israel Hands seemed suspicious.

But just then a sort of brightness fell upon us, and looking up, I found the moon had risen and was shining white on the luff of the fore-sail; and almost at the same time the voice of the lookout shouted, "Land ho!"

There was a great rush of feet across the deck. I could hear people tumbling up from the cabin and the forecastle. Could it really be that we had found Treasure Island at last?

All hands congregated at the bow; many stared into the distance at the land that had just been sighted. A belt of fog had lifted almost simultaneously with the appearance of the moon. Away to the southwest of us we saw two low hills, a couple of miles apart, and rising behind one of them a third and higher hill, whose peak was still buried in the fog. All three seemed sharp and conical in figure.

"Has any one of you ever seen that land ahead?" asked the captain.

"I have, sir," said Silver. "I've watered there with a trader I was cook in. Skeleton Island, they calls it. It were a main place for pirates once. That hill to the north they call Fore-mast Hill; and then the three hills run southward—fore, main, and mizzen, sir. But the main—that's the big un, with the cloud on it—they usually calls the Spy-glass, by reason of a lookout they kept there when they cleaned their ships, sir."

"I have a chart here," says the captain. "See if that's the place."

Long John's eyes burned in his head as he took the chart, but by the fresh look of the paper I knew he was doomed to disappointment. This was not the map I found in Billy Bones's chest, but an accurate copy, complete in all things—names and heights and soundings—with the single exception of the red crosses and the written notes. He must have been so annoyed, but Silver had the strength of mind to hide it.

"Yes, sir," said he, "this is the spot, to be sure."

"Thank you," said Captain Smollett. "You may go."

He bowed his head to the captain and then moved away, passing by me and giving me a conspiratorial smile.

"It won't be long now, Jimmy. You were wise to join us. You've earned yourself a larger share of the treasure, and your mortal life as well, eh?" He laughed wickedly and went down to the galley.

With Silver gone, I knew I had to tell my friends that I now had proof of the sea-cook's treachery. I searched the deck for my friends and was delighted by what I found.

Turn to page 145

felt nervous to join the three men at their table. The situation was grave, and their expressions were grim. But then they poured me drink and fed me, toasted to my good health, and pledged their service to me for my luck and courage.

"Now, Captain," said the squire, "you were right, and I was wrong. I am a fool, and I await your orders."

"No more a fool than I, sir," returned the captain. "I never heard of a crew that meant to mutiny but what showed signs before, but this crew beats me."

"That's Silver's doing," said the doctor. "A remarkable man."

"A few points," began Captain Smollett. "We must go on. If we turned the ship back, the crew would rise at once. And second, we have time—at least until the treasure is found. Third, some of the men are faithful to us. It will come to blows sooner or later, but let us wait until some fine day when they least expect it. Mr. Trelawney, can we count on your own home servants?"

"As upon myself," declared the squire.

"Three," reckoned the captain; "ourselves makes seven, counting Hawkins here. Now, about the honest hands."

"Most likely Trelawney's own men," said the doctor; "those he picked up before he lit on Silver."

"Nay," replied the squire. "Israel Hands was one of mine. And to think that they're all Englishmen!" he broke out. "Sir, I could find it in my heart to blow the ship up."

"Well, gentlemen," said the captain, "the best I can say is to keep a bright lookout."

"Jim will be of great help," said the doctor. "The men are not shy with him, and he is a noticing lad."

"Hawkins, I put prodigious faith in you," added the squire.

I found this all quite ironic, as I felt altogether helpless, yet it was through me that safety came. But little safety would I provide. Of the twenty-six souls aboard the *Hispaniola*, only on seven could we rely, and one of those seven was a boy, so six grown men to their nineteen.

Turn to page 187

*L*ong John Silver wanted me to take a guess as to how the first mate, Mr. Arrow, met his demise, but I had long since made up my mind about the poor wretch's outcome.

I said, "You see, sirs, I believe that Mr. Arrow was the finest, most upstanding gentleman aboard the *Hispaniola*."

"Impossible!" snorted one of the sailors. "Some days he never left his bunk. How can you say such a fable?"

"Because I believe our Mr. Arrow was *poisoned*," I snapped, silencing the room. "That's right. I believe someone aboard this ship slipped rum to Mr. Arrow, but the rum was laced with something even more nefarious and intoxicating. It made Mr. Arrow disoriented and unlike himself. He would frequently cut himself when he was in one of his stupors. Who *cuts* himself when he's had a few swigs of rum, my friends? Once the man had been thoroughly sabotaged, it would be trivial to nudge him overboard in the dead of night while most of the crew slept. Think of it, men!"

"What cause would one of our own have to assassinate the first mate?" asked Long John Silver nervously.

"I know not," I confessed. "But we may all be in danger. We don't know who's next!"

Then suddenly the men burst into uproarious laughter. "Who would want to kill that miserable drunk, Mr. Arrow?" asked one of the men. "He was a waste of space, but that wouldn't justify offing the poor chap."

The others howled in amusement as well, slapping the tables and snorting like farm swine, and yet there was something about their derision. I noticed the men exchange furtive glances, and I wondered if they had other thoughts that they did not let on.

Turn to page 136

*I*t was not my business what Mr. Arrow did with his idle time, though I wish from the very bottom of my mortal soul that I had intervened in some way, for he was not only useless as an officer and a bad influence among the men, but it was plain that at this rate he would soon kill himself outright, so nobody was much surprised, nor very sorry, when one dark night, with a head sea, he disappeared entirely and was seen no more.

"Overboard!" said the captain. "Well, gentlemen, that saves the trouble of putting him in irons."

In the galley, I heard the men share their own speculations. "Fell overboard? Not likely. The man never left his bunk, the lazy sod. I wager a sea-witch shrank him down to nothing!"

Another sailor laughed as he spooned down a stew Long John Silver had prepared. "I'll take that wager. I know he caught aflame and burned to nothing. What do they call it? Spontaneous combustion!"

"That's what we all do after a breakfast of Mr. Silver's beans!" cawed a third.

"I think Mr. Arrow was struck by lightning!"

"He's still aboard, but in disguise!"

"What about you, Jim?" asked Long John Silver as he ladled out more stew for the men. "Surely you have a theory about what happened to our dearly departed Mr. Arrow."

"Me, sir?" said I. "I'm not sure."

"Well, go on, at least," encouraged the ship's cook. "Take a guess."

I considered it and decided to tell the men what I thought happened to Mr. Arrow.

If you think Mr. Arrow got drunk and fell overboard, turn to page 159

If you think Mr. Arrow was murdered by pirates, turn to page 183

If you think Mr. Arrow was abducted by mermaids, turn to page 34

The appearance of the island when I came on deck the next morning was altogether changed. Although the breeze had now utterly ceased, we had made a great deal of way during the night and were now lying becalmed about half a mile to the southeast of the island's low eastern coast. Gray, melancholy woods covered a large part of the surface, and from my first look onward, I hated the very thought of Treasure Island.

We had a dreary morning's work before us, for there was no sign of any wind. The small boats were manned and pulled the *Hispaniola* round to the haven where we would lay anchor. The heat was sweltering, and the men grumbled fiercely over their work. Anderson was in command of my boat, and instead of keeping the crew in order, he grumbled as loud as the worst.

"Well, at least it's not forever," he said with an oath.

I thought this was a very bad sign, for up to that day the

men had gone briskly and willingly about their business; but the very sight of the island had relaxed the cords of discipline.

When the work was done, the men lay about the deck growling together in talk. The slightest order was received with a black look and grudgingly and carelessly obeyed. Even the honest hands must have caught the infection, for there was not one man aboard to mend another. Mutiny, it was plain, hung over us like a thundercloud.

But Long John was hard at work going from group to group, outstripping himself in willingness and civility; he was all smiles to everyone. If an order was given, John would be on his crutch in an instant, with the cheeriest "Aye, aye, sir!" in the world. When there was nothing else to do, he kept up one song after another, as if to conceal the discontent of the rest. To me, Long John's kindness was the scariest thing about our whole predicament.

We held a council in the cabin.

"Sir," said the captain, "if I risk another order, it's all over. No matter what, I'll get a rough answer. If I speak back, the men will revolt; if I don't, Silver will see there's something under that, and the game's up. There's only one man left to rely on."

"And who's that?" asked the squire.

"Long John Silver," returned the captain. "He'd talk the men down if he had the chance, so let's give him the chance.

Let's allow the men an afternoon ashore. Silver'll bring 'em aboard again as mild as lambs."

It was so decided; loaded pistols were served out to all the sure men; Hunter, Joyce, and Redruth were taken into our confidence and received the news with less surprise and a better spirit than we had looked for, and then the captain addressed the crew.

"My lads, it's been a hot day and we are all tired. A turn ashore'll hurt nobody—take the boats and as many as please may go ashore for the afternoon. I'll fire a gun half an hour before sundown."

The silly fellows must have thought they would break their shins over treasure as soon as they were landed, for they all came out of their sulks in a moment and gave a cheer that started an echo in a faraway hill and sent the birds flying and squalling round the anchorage.

The captain stayed out of the way, leaving Silver to arrange the party. Had he stayed, he could not have pretended not to understand the situation. It was as plain as day. Silver was the captain, and a mighty rebellious crew he had of it. When at last the party was made up, six fellows were to stay on board, and the remaining thirteen, including Silver, began to embark.

Then it was that there came into my head a rather wild notion. With six of Silver's men left on board, our party could not fight and take the ship. So they would have no need of me.

I could go ashore myself and see what mischief the pirates would get up to.

If you would go ashore,
turn to page 169

If you would stay aboard the ship,
turn to page 67